UNWILLING AND DEFIANT

A STANDALONE REJECTED MATE ALPHA SHIFTERS
NOVELLA

CLAIMED

BOOK THREE

CHRISTINA MATTINGLY

CONTENT AND TRIGGER WARNINGS

Stalking, possessive behavior, jealousy, knotting, imprinting, multiple partners, TTC, power dynamics,

Tropes and tags: He falls first, BDSM, TTC, imprinting
    Pairings: MF, FF

MAP OF PINEHURST

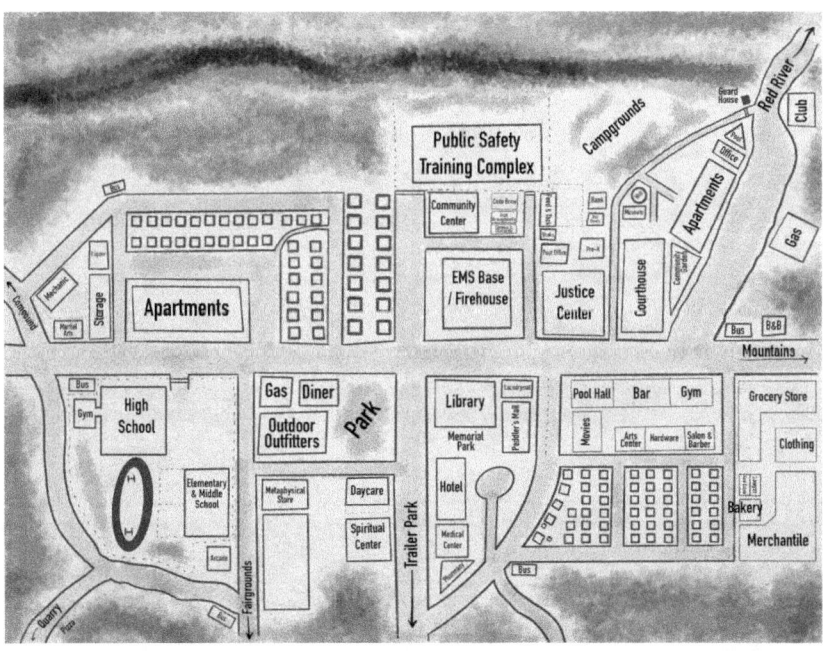

CHAPTER ONE

CALEN

"Oou don't need to apologize." A tall, powerfully built man with salt and pepper hair leaned back on the desk cut from oaks in the forest just beyond the limits of his small town of Pinehurst.

"I don't want to get anyone in trouble," she said again, stealing a guilty glance at Calen.

"You did the right thing coming to discuss it with Miss Linda," Jason said, running a finger through his already-tousled hair. "Now, head on to the kitchen. She'll make you a cup of tea and ensure you get home safely. Unless there's anything else either of you wanted to add?"

"I'm sorry," Calen said, the words thick in his mouth as he fought to hold down the dinner he'd eaten hastily on the way over.

He had thought maybe Miss Linda needed a hand with something. All of the biological alpha wolf shifters in the pack were on speed dial for her in case she needed something and the Alpha wasn't available. What he didn't expect was for Julie, his full moon companion from a few days before, to be sitting in the Alpha's study, crying.

When they first caught sight of her, Calen's wolf Ryne gave a little yip of recognition, then a low rumbling growl. She wasn't theirs, but some-

1

thing had clearly happened to this little omega, and they'd been with her. She was a member of the pack, and they weren't the type of man and wolf that mated with a female under the full moon and didn't care about her after. Whoever had hurt her would pay at Calen's hands or Ryne's teeth.

As her story had unfolded, the food Calen had eaten on his way to the alpha's house had turned to lead, his wolf falling silent in shock and horror.

Her story was that she'd met Calen in the Bar on Main, they'd hit it off. She was an omega who wanted to be dominated in every way, a true masochist who wanted a lot of pain with her pleasure. She wanted to try having a biological alpha male to add another layer of domination to her sex, and Calen had been happy to comply.

They'd had a discussion about expectations, limits, and her desires. He had been careful to note them and to make sure she was clear on her safe words. Then he'd done exactly as she asked, or he'd intended to.

Her claim was that he'd overpowered her, that his wolf's dominance had been too much, and he'd pushed her far past what she could handle, and he'd dominated her so completely, that she couldn't use her safe word. Calen had listened to her talk, horror growing. She had no reason to lie, and the Alpha's magic compelled them both to tell the truth in any case. She insisted she couldn't use her safe word, while Calen insisted that he would never proceed with anything if he felt she couldn't give, or withdraw, consent.

Once Julie left the study, Calen stood and walked around to the trash can that sat behind Jason's desk. Grabbing it, Calen hurled the contents of his dinner, his stomach heaving until there was only bile left to expel. When he'd emptied his stomach, he took the trash bag and tied it, setting it on the floor by the study door.

"Chief," Calen began. "I would never hurt a girl. I mean, not like that. Not like what she said. I know she wasn't lying, but neither was I."

"I believe you, son. I know you weren't lying. I know you didn't want to harm her. Believe me, if you had, this would not be a friendly discussion. I take the safety and well-being of every member of my pack very seriously, especially the omegas."

Calen nodded and the older man tilted his head.

"Do you know what you could have done differently?" The chief asked, handing him a bottle of water from the mini-fridge tucked away in one of the cabinets that were part of the study's built-in bookshelves.

Calen shook his head, clearing the acidic taste from his mouth. He'd done everything right, except it had all gone horribly wrong.

"You let too much of your wolf out with an omega," the chief said, not unkindly. "I know it doesn't make it any better, but it happens, especially with omegas. If she'd been another alpha or a beta, she probably would have been able to speak up. This is part of learning how to control being a biological alpha, son."

The words sank into Calen's mind, but he still felt removed from the situation, like he was in shock. His alpha continued, reaching out to put a hand on Calen's shoulder.

"Unfortunately, sometimes we have to learn by making these mistakes. This is one you'll never make again. Normally it happens with another pack member, and I regret that it happened in an intimate setting. I know that's difficult to live with, but Julie will be fine. Next time you know to be more careful, especially in an intimate setting."

Calen nodded, and Ryne's mental voice finally spoke into his mind.

We need to go. To run. Now.

Calen didn't bother to fight it. All he wanted was to shed his clothing. His fingers moved almost of their own accord, unbuttoning his shirt, knowing the chief would understand.

"I need to... go," Calen said, rising. "Can I leave my truck here?"

"I'll tell your captain not to expect you in tomorrow. Take the day, take a few days if you need to, get your head on straight. Come back when you and Ryne are ready."

Calen nodded and stripped down to the base layer he kept on that would stay intact as he shifted, magically adhering to his skin so that when he shifted back, he wouldn't be completely nude.

Without another word, Calen stripped out of his clothes and stood in his base layer, then shifted without another word. The alpha opened one of the double doors that led to the backyard, with a place cut out of the back fence the perfect size for a grown wolf to slip through to the track that led through to the mountains.

Calen let Ryne take control, running until their mind was blissfully blank. He wasn't sure how to make this right, but he would make damn sure it would never happen again.

CHAPTER TWO

CALEN

FOUR MONTHS LATER

*T*he girl from last night was still in the bed when Calen woke from his post-coital rest. Sleep after taking an enthusiastic partner to bed on the full moon was the best kind of rest. Pinehurst was a small town with a disproportionate amount of shifters and fae. Calen never lacked for partners, but it was nice when your hookup for the night could match your energy.

He'd worked a thirty-six-hour shift and hadn't bothered to do anything but grab a shower, change out of his paramedic's uniform, and head to The Bar on Main, the only bar in Pinehurst. The bar was packed, as it normally was on the full moon, and he'd barely walked into the bar when a tall beauty with long, straight black hair pulled back in a braid had strode forward and asked him if he was looking for company. He'd said yes and asked if she wanted to go to his place or hers.

She'd followed him home in her car, and less than five minutes later, she'd been naked in his bed. He'd taken her from behind, careful not to be too rough with her, reveling in her sounds of pleasure.

Interrupting his replaying of the night before, the girl in his bed sighed and brought his mind back to the present. The smell of her arousal could have been what woke him. Their scents mingled in the bed, but he could still smell her proof of a fresh wave of desire, her body calling to his in the way only another shifter's could.

Listening to her breathing for a moment, he realized she was also awake. He waited to see if she would stir, but she laid still. Maybe she wasn't used to being with an alpha, or maybe she'd been with some of the other bio alphas who lived in Pinehurst who had some bullshit rules about them being the only ones allowed to initiate sex, because 'they were the 'leaders' in bed.'

Calen preferred his women feisty, and if you had to declare just how dominant you were, then you were a shitty dominant, whether it was a matter of bedroom dynamics or just dealing with other people in general. Calen looked at the back of her head, her hair a mess from where he'd buried his fingers in it the night before, and waited to give her an opportunity to make the first move, if she wanted to.

She'd been bold in the bar last night, walking right up to him and asking him if he wanted to leave, but maybe he'd been too much for her and accidentally intimidated her. He suppressed a sigh at the thought, and his wolf growled through their mental link at the idea. Both he and Ryne wanted a partner who he didn't have to hold back with, someone who could match their energy on the full moon and he wouldn't have to worry about damaging or intimidating.

She was lying on her right side with her back to him, long, dark, straight hair in a wild cascade down her back. Rolling over, he sidled up to her, putting his hand on her hip. She surprised him by grabbing his hand and sliding it around her middle, scooting back against him so her naked back was pressed to his chest, angling her hips away slightly so she didn't brush against his erection.

"Shhhhh," she soothed him, stroking his arm, and snuggling against him. "I'm not going anywhere."

Her voice was hypnotic and laced with magic and gentle authority that soothed his wolf into a drowsy state for several moments before he realized what was going on. She wasn't coming onto him like a full moon partner normally would. She was trying to pacify him, and it was working.

Ryne perked up, growling indignantly at someone else using their magic on them. The only way that she would be able to do that is if she had some kind of magic, or she was a biological alpha herself. He'd been so focused on the sex and holding his wolf back from overwhelming her, that he had noticed nothing about her wolf's energy.

He looked over her shoulder, surprised to see her phone in her hand. The screen was black. Her brightness must have been turned all the way down. She scrolled, then stopped. His eyes focused on the barely visible screen. The entire screen was filled with words. He felt a flood of jealousy that something other than him would arouse her on the full moon, then curiosity won over and he read, in fascinating detail, a highly erotic sex scene.

She shifted her body a few times, blowing out her breath quietly as her arousal built, his nose filling with her scent. She was so aroused, that he could probably have buried himself to the hilt with one thrust.

He wondered why she hadn't woken him - most shifter women went crazy for any sex during the full moon, alphas even more so, if indeed she was an alpha. Her magic didn't have that foreign, slightly metallic tang that fae magic did, so he figured she was most likely a shifter as well. Pulling closer to her, he let his wolf rumble at her, deep and low in her ear. She clicked off her phone, sliding it under the pillow.

"I wasn't done with that. I wanted to know what he does once he's done licking her," he teased. She rolled over toward him, having the decency to blush.

"I couldn't sleep," she explained, lifting her head to free the long strands of straight brown hair that had escaped the braid she'd had it in the night before and were trapped beneath her.

"I could have helped you with that."

Calen wasn't accustomed to a woman being anything other than enthusiastic because of his lucky genes. Since shifters lived in such close proximity, often mating with the fae, there were some shifters who, for no apparent reason, would be born as alphas.

As a biological alpha, you had a few choices. You could integrate into a pack, submitting to the current alpha, challenge the pack's alpha and claim the pack for yourself, or leave and go start your own pack. Calen had grown up as part of the Pinehurst pack and was content to stay that way. He was content managing his jobs: working as a paramedic and doing truck maintenance for the county's ambulances and fire and rescue vehicles.

A brief flash of something that looked awfully close to skepticism crossed her face.

"I was fine reading," she replied.

"You were fine? You shouldn't be fine, you should be amazing."

"Not every full moon is amazing for everyone, but hey- it's no big deal. It's okay for it to be just fine." She smiled, then looked at his body with carnal appreciation. "You up for another round before I go?"

Had she just implied that last night hadn't been amazing? That it had been just fine? Ryne growled as Calen settled for leaning in to kiss her, but she put a restraining hand on his chest.

"Two seconds."

She winked, then scampered off to the bathroom while he lay there, resting up on one elbow as he mulled over what she'd said.

Just fine. She'd meant last night had been just fine- that's all he'd been. Ryne growled at the idea that she hadn't been satisfied.

He thought back, running through every touch, every moment, frowning. She'd orgasmed- he remembered it vividly. It had been real, hadn't it? Surely she hadn't faked it with him. The idea made him feel slightly sick.

What was she on about? By the time she came back to the bedroom, his wolf had nearly convinced him that it didn't matter that she'd thought it was *just fine*. They could convince her otherwise with actions. But he held off. His wolf may want to blindly mate, but his human ego was getting in the way.

"You didn't enjoy last night?" He couldn't leave it alone.

"It was nice," she replied with a polite smile.

"Nice?"

"Yeah. I'd recommend you to a friend," she said, laying back down on the bed, looking at him expectantly.

"Um."

"Unless you don't want to," she started to rise.

"No."

He grabbed her hip, turning her towards him possessively. It wasn't appropriate for him to be possessive with a female he had no understanding with, but Ryne was so incensed at the idea that she had faked an orgasm with him that Calen couldn't resist him and didn't want to. Her look turned cold, her lip curling up in a silent snarl of rebuke, the irises of her blue eyes growing dark as her wolf made its presence known. She didn't accept his dominance and wouldn't tolerate possessive behavior.

Her resistance fascinated him and made him pause, Ryne stilling inside Calen's mind, held captive by her energy. They'd never had a woman stand up to them when they genuinely wanted to dominate her. Not that he'd intended to do anything she didn't want, but the sheer fact that she *could* resist stopped them both in their tracks.

With a firm grip, she removed his hand from her hip, then putting her hand on his chest, applied firm pressure until he ceded control to her, lying flat on his back. She straddled him, rubbing herself against him, tongue held between her teeth as she allowed him to enter her, sinking down on his cock so he filled her.

Calen went to put his hands on her hips, but she stopped him with a look of warning, so he rested them on her thighs tentatively. Ryne was letting out a low, rolling growl, marveling at a woman whose wolf could match his energy, and wanting to take over and subdue her, but being completely spellbound and unable to do a thing as she used Calen's body for her own pleasure.

Calen, Ryne half-whined, half-growled. *She's challenging us.*

She doesn't want us to take control, Calen thought back as they watched her ride him, his cock aching to release inside of her hot, wet core.

I beg to differ, Ryne challenged darkly.

And if you're wrong? Calen thought back.

Inside Calen's head, Ryne was silent and sullen, offering no reply but his simmering frustration. Accepting Calen's decision, he watched as the girl rode Calen with practiced ease, their minds a swirl of confusion and wonder.

She wasn't just posturing; she had taken control, and they'd let her. Never had he encountered a woman, wolf, human, or fae, who had the force of will to do that to him outside of their pack's true alpha. By the moon, she was perfect.

When she ground herself against him with her pussy gripping his cock like a vise. He reveled in her pleasure until he realized she wasn't looking at him, wasn't reacting to him. She was using his body to get herself off like he was there to service her, not the other way around.

While it was true that full moon matings were there to meet each other's needs, Calen had never been the kind of lover who intended to leave his lover wanting. But, typically, when a girl sought an alpha male to enjoy for the night, she desired to be used, not the other way around. And this girl had definitely known. She'd looked into his eyes, straddled him, and taken control like it was her right.

He may have been thinking about his cock too much to pay attention to her wolf and the energy she gave off last night, but he was paying attention now, and he was done with this.

Oh, hell no. He moved his hands to grip her hips and show her just where she lay in the pack order when she came loudly, digging her nails into his chest, marking him.

She fell onto the bed, dragging his arm, so he followed.

"Now you."

He took half a second to look at her in exasperation. She'd used him. His wolf let out a growl. He got on top of her, pounding into her. He worked furiously, trying to get a reaction, to make her come again, but she reacted just enough to be polite, no matter what he did.

"I'm good if you're trying to…" she trailed off delicately.

He gave her an exasperated huff, but she smiled serenely in response. He did come inside of her, but the pleasure was gone. He rolled away but kept his eyes on her. She rose to get dressed.

It was the first time since he'd started participating in full moon matings that he hadn't had a woman cling to him, or want to.

"You don't want breakfast?"

If you brought someone home for the full moon, it was considerate to have breakfast. It wasn't a hard and fast rule, but it was one of the courtesies he liked to observe. Usually, both parties had worked up such an appetite by morning that breakfast was a necessity. Here she was, almost completely unfazed.

"No, thanks," she replied as she pulled on her pants.

"Do you have to work early?"

What was the matter with him? Wasn't this what he was always hoping for- a woman who wasn't clingy and hoping for a future with a biological alpha?

As she put on her bra and shirt, he gritted his teeth. He needed to get it together.

"Your underwear is in here somewhere," he grabbed the blankets, sifting through them.

"Don't worry about it. Enjoy the souvenir."

The irony that he'd said something similar to a number of girls about various articles of his own clothing wasn't lost on him. And just like that, she wiggled her fingers while he lay there trying to think of something to say. He moved off the bed, pulling on his pants as he tried to form a coherent thought.

When he looked up, she was gone. He cursed when he realized he didn't even know her name.

CHAPTER THREE

CHEYENNE

*C*heyenne couldn't get out of there fast enough. Last night had been disappointing, to say the least. Making her way to the parking lot of the apartment complex, she stopped next to her car, sighing. She needed a shower. Other girls she'd spoken to had praised Calen Merrick as a passionate lover and a genuine alpha, but he'd been a huge letdown, one she was becoming all too familiar with.

She'd been working her way through Pinehurst's short list of single shifters who'd been born with the genes of an alpha wolf, and Calen had been the last one. She sighed again, opening her phone's fertility tracker and logging unprotected sex last night and this morning. If she didn't do it before she got in the car, she would forget.

"Hey you," a familiar voice sounded from the vehicle, parked a few parking spots down from hers.

Matt Griffith stood there, the top two buttons of his work shirt unbuttoned, his breath coming out in white puffs in the cool January morning air. Sunrise was a few hours away yet, and she swallowed hard. Her wolf Hazel perked up as Cheyenne's eyes wandered over his body, his chocolate-colored eyes lighting up as he noticed her interest.

With a single heated look, Matt reminded her of the time left before sunrise as he adjusted his backpack. Moisture leaked from her as her body responded. Her arousal mingled with Calen's seed soaking her panties. One of the many benefits of being a female shifter: she was always ready to go on the full moon.

"Hey, Matt!"

Before she'd decided to get pregnant and go for an alpha male with the hopes that she would meet someone whose energy matched her wolf's, she'd spent time with Matt during a few full moons and he'd come into her work almost every month, like lots of the local shifter guys, to have fruit arrangements delivered to the lady they'd spent the night with the evening before. They'd become pretty friendly during the last year. Not the best of friends, but there was definitely chemistry there, even when the moon wasn't full.

Matt was a nice guy. As a beta, he wasn't quite as dominant as she may prefer, but he was a far cry more dominant than the supposed alpha's bed she'd just emerged from.

"Where are you coming from?" Matt asked casually as he clicked the button on his fob that locked his truck.

"304," she said.

"Ah yeah. Calen's a great guy," Matt replied, looking her over.

"Mm," she said noncommittally, searching in her purse for her car keys.

"Didn't have a good time?" Matt asked, walking closer.

Cheyenne paused, trying to think of a polite response as her whole body responded to his nearness with a primal need to be dominated and fucked hard.

"It was fine."

"Ouch," he laughed, looking at his own keys to find his house key. When he looked up, her eyes were on him with a hungry longing that made his hands still.

"You wanna come in and shower?" He asked, tilting his head toward the house.

It wasn't polite to solicit a woman after she'd already paired with someone else for the full moon, but offering a shower was perfectly within social bounds. Sex inside the shower was implied, but it was an offer that she could politely decline.

"I'd love that."

She barely let him make it in the front door before her hands were on him, pulling at his clothes, huffing impatiently at the inconvenience of his buttons, belt, and zipper.

"Fuck, Cheyenne," he murmured as she went to unbutton his pants, then slid a hand inside, wrapping them around his semi-hard cock.

He chuckled, sliding his pants and boxers down, giving her easier access.

"God, yes," Matt groaned.

Cheyenne worked his cock with one hand as he grabbed the front of her jeans, using the front panels by her zipper to pull her with him as he walked backwards into the bathroom, turning on the hot water with one hand while she worked his shaft.

She only released him to strip off her top, and she enjoyed how his eyes flitted over her naked breasts, approving of the fact that she hadn't bothered with a bra last night, so there was one less piece of clothing to remove. Shimmying out of her jeans, she dropped to her knees and took him in her mouth.

He wasn't fully erect, but it took almost nothing before he was hard as a rock inside of her hot mouth. She sucked eagerly, her head bobbing as she went down on him like it was the only thing keeping her alive.

He held his hand out, testing the water, adjusting it slightly as she sucked him, then when it felt fine he grabbed the back of her hair, pulling her off his cock with an audible sucking sound. He dragged her to her feet and into the shower with him.

"Need me to be gentle with you?" He murmured.

They had hooked up plenty of times. He knew her body well, but he didn't know how rough Merrick might have been with her and he didn't want to hurt her if she was already tender.

"You know how I like it," she answered against this mouth.

His hands still tangled in her hair, he pulled her in for a rough kiss.

"Good girl," he crooned, using his free hand to slide between her legs. "You don't feel like you have enough cum inside of you, baby. Wasn't Calen good to your pussy last night?"

"Not really," she complained.

"Aw, we'll have to fix that," he said.

She was so worked up he barely had to do anything and she was almost coming, but he didn't let her. Instead, he used his fingers to edge her, bringing her to the brink until finally, she whined with need.

"Matt," she whined as he swirled his finger inside of her, her hands roving his chest desperately. "That's mean."

"Do you want me to stop?" He asked with a sadistic grin.

"No," she said, giving him a pouting glare.

"I didn't think so," he smirked.

He slid his fingers inside of her and immediately she came around him, her pussy clamping down on his fingers.

"You're so tight," he murmured as his fingers slipped out of her.

Her orgasm fizzled, and she groaned, letting her head fall back against the wall of the shower with a thud.

"Aw, does my good girl need more?" He asked in a low, teasing voice.

"Yes, please, Matt, I need more," Cheyenne said.

"What do you need more of, baby girl?" he asked.

"I need you to make me cum really hard. I need it so bad," she begged, her eyes desperate.

"You're a needy thing this morning," he observed.

As soon as his fingers were at her entrance again, he chuckled.

"You're so fucking tight, I'm just gonna have to force my fingers in there," he said.

She cried out as he did exactly that, stretching her and filling her with his fingers until she was nearly delirious with the need to orgasm. He filled her with his fingers, hard enough that she would surely feel it later.

"Come for me, baby."

15

Her orgasm ripped through her like a hurricane, tearing a scream of ecstasy from her lips as pleasure shot through her body.

"Good girl," Matt praised as she came, his voice heavy with satisfaction.

As she came back down, her eyes found his. He was grinning at her, observing her with satisfaction, and she laughed.

"You have no idea how much I needed that."

"Oh, I felt it all. I know," he replied. "I thought you were gonna break my fingers."

She smiled a touch shyly.

"That what you needed?" Matt asked, regarding her.

She shook her head.

"I mean, yes, that was lovely," she said. "But I was hoping for actual sex."

"Mm-kay," he murmured before leaning forward to kiss her. "Tell me exactly what you need."

"I need your cum inside of me, please."

"Do you?"

"Yes, please," she pleaded, leaning forward to bite his neck hard enough that he sucked his breath in through his teeth, yanking her hair back.

"Ask nicely, like a good girl," he demanded.

"Fuck my pussy and fill me with your cum," she replied, her eyes shining with sassy impertinence.

"Ask nicely or I'll fuck your throat raw and your pussy won't get any of my cum," he threatened.

"Please, please fuck my pussy," she whined, her eyes wild with need.

Sunrise was still a few hours off, her body was still very much under the effects of the moon. She was desperate to be fucked, everything within her crying out to be bred.

"Okay, baby."

She turned around, bent over, and put her hands on the edge of the tub. He positioned his cock at her entrance. She pushed back, taking all of him at once, taking Matt by surprise, who let out a low groan as his grip on her hips. She was wet from her own arousal and Calen's attentions and he slid inside easily.

He began thrusting, his cock threatening to explode after only a few strokes.

"Hurt me," she begged.

He grabbed her hair again, using it to yank her head back as he thrust deep, jerking her head backward with one hand on her hip, the other in her hair. She screamed as her walls gripped his cock, making him grunt as he emptied himself into her.

They were both panting as he withdrew. Cheyenne turned back to face him, red-faced, and laughed a little.

"Feel better?" he asked.

"Much," she agreed.

"I don't have anywhere to be this morning. I just worked the night shift. If you wanna go another round and have a bite before you go, you're welcome to stay," he said, leaning against the shower wall.

"Yeah?"

"Yup."

"I would love that," she breathed, offering him a grateful smile.

After their brief shower, they didn't make it to the bedroom before he'd pushed her up against the wall, spreading her cheeks and shoving his cock deep inside of her.

"You're a needy girl today," he murmured. "Why is that?"

"I want to have a baby," she panted as he took her with considerable force.

"Do you? Do you want me to breed you tonight?"

"I take out my birth control implant tomorrow, or I guess now that's later on today."

"So, what you're saying is, I could be fucking a baby in you right now," he said in her ear.

"Yes," she breathed.

"Do you want that?" he was filling her with slow, gentle movements as they spoke.

"Yeah, I do," she said.

"Good," he grunted and thrust deep, burying himself deep in her and thrusting his hips forward. He emptied himself inside of her again. "I'm gonna wear your pussy out, fucking my baby into you."

CHAPTER FOUR

CALEN

*C*alen was going to be late for his shift. He'd showered and dressed, eating the breakfast he normally would have politely shared with his full-moon companion. Now he scarfed the food down, barely noticing the taste, growling in displeasure every time he replayed the events of the early morning.

When genes of humans, fae, and shifters mixed, most females ended with stronger fae traits, while the males ended with shifter traits. Female shifters, like the one from last night, were uncommon, but to have alpha genetics mixed in was almost unheard of. Last night, he'd been so shocked when her wolf's dominance matched his own, he'd felt stuck.

He wondered how it would have felt to unleash himself last night. Most women's subconscious felt delicate. The girl from last night though, he wondered if she could have handled the intensity of Ryne's dominance full-on. He had to adjust his erection as he grew hard at the idea, his wolf grumbling in frustration.

He should have talked with her more before they jumped into bed, talked about limits, but he hadn't, and she'd left before he'd caught her name. Calen grumbled along with his wolf and grabbed his keys, heading out the door. He may as well go in early and work on one of the trucks since there was no way he was going back to sleep. Anything was better than sitting around chasing his tail.

Dressed in his grungy clothes he used when he was working on the trucks, Calen threw his uniform in a bag for when he clocked in for his twenty-four-hour shift as a firefighter. He headed out to his truck, shivering in the crisp February air.

We could be in bed with that girl, Ryne pointed out. *If you had-*

You don't think I'm not painfully aware of that? Calen snapped.

Sorry, his wolf amended.

Fuck. Me too. Calen thought back, his chest tightening as he heard a familiar voice that interrupted his thoughts.

"Oh, fuck- Matt!" It was definitely the girl from last night. Calen gripped his keys.

She went to another man? His wolf demanded.

Looking around, he spotted his neighbor's bathroom window, the top glass lowered so steam poured out of the window along with her sounds of ecstasy. Failing to satisfy a woman on the full moon was something that Calen hadn't experienced.

He wasn't the type to leave a female wanting, even if he didn't want to keep them around forever. There was a big difference between not wanting to live with a woman for the rest of your life and being that guy who couldn't even satisfy a girl for one night. He didn't want a mate, but he sure as hell wasn't settling for *just fine* or *nice.* Fuck that.

"Gods," her voice was rising again with unrestrained pleasure.

She certainly hadn't sounded like that last night. Calen tried to block out the sounds as he stomped to his truck and the images of what exactly his coworker might be doing to her to get that kind of reaction. Calen closed his truck door harder than necessary, jamming his key in the ignition before he lost his temper.

This is stupid, he chastised himself.

She's just a girl, his wolf reminded him.

BY THE TIME he got to work, he'd mostly shaken it off. One girl, that's all she was. One unimportant girl who hadn't had a good time. That happened to lots of guys. It was no big deal. It hadn't ever happened to him and Ryne, but it was fine.

You can't win them all, Calen thought.

Yup. We'll find another girl and rock her world on your next day off, Ryne said supportively.

Rolling into the station, he headed for the office. Looking over the truck repair list, he sighed in frustration and got to work. As his hands moved to access the parts for one of the ambulances, his mind wandered back to last night's girl.

He thought she'd had a nice time. Hell, he'd worked hard to make sure he wasn't overbearing for a first time. He wasn't sure when he'd decided it was a first-time coupling instead of a one-time event, but of that he was certain.

Calen came to a stopping point and went to grab the clipboard to check the last time this particular truck had been in for service, but he stared at the clipboard and all he could think about was the girl from last night and how she'd sounded in the shower with Matt.

"Got something on your mind?" A voice sounded from behind him, startling Calen.

"Nothing, chief."

"Well, nothing's bending my clipboard," the chief noted, his voice tinged with amusement.

"Oh, sorry," Calen huffed at himself, bending the metal clipboard back, grimacing when it looked worse than before.

"I'm not worried about that. What's on your mind, son?"

All biological alphas had regular meetings with the alpha when you lived in his territory. Some pack leaders used it as an excuse to reinforce their authority and dominance, but the chief used it to keep a finger on the pulse of the community, taking notes on community programs and problems to be looked into, and issues that could be solved.

"Have you ever had a woman you didn't satisfy? I mean, it's never happened to me before. She was..." he shook his head, "Ever since,

21

you know, I've been careful to hold back. I don't want to hurt a girl who can't handle Ryne full-on."

"I remember those days," the chief agreed.

"But with her, she just sort of- I don't know how to describe it. I was there and she just sort of took charge. She…" Calen shrugged.

"Deactivated you?"

"Yeah!"

"Mm-hmm. I had that happen once." His alpha nodded with a sigh, looking out into the bay, and seeing something in the past.

"What did you do?"

"I courted her for two years before I convinced her to be my mate." The chief grinned.

"Two *years?*" Calen asked, surprised.

"Mm-hmm. That stubborn woman made me work for every inch of ground I gained. Damn near drove me feral," he grinned at the memory, shaking his head, his eyes returning to the present.

"Was it worth it?"

Two years was a long time to go after a woman, by human, fae, or shifter standards.

"Are you asking me if it was worth it to court my wife of over twenty years?" He asked with an ironic raise of an eyebrow.

"Yes." Calen met the alpha's eye briefly then dropped his gaze, not wanting to challenge him, but also needing the older man to see that he was sincere and had no intention of disrespect.

"I couldn't do what I do without her. She makes everything worth it, all the bullshit and the late nights taking care of the pack business and bullshit. I wouldn't be half the man I am today without her."

"Have any advice?"

The chief thought about it, sizing up Calen.

"Let your wolf handle things."

"Yeah?"

Definitely not the advice Calen was expecting.

"Mm-hmm. You keep your human brain out too much. You'll overthink it and mess it up," Jason advised.

"Okay," Calen nodded, then spoke up, "Can I ask something personal, chief?"

"You already have, but go ahead."

"A two-year courtship… that's a long time."

"That's not a question."

"Why was it so long?"

"She wasn't entirely agreeable to the idea initially."

Calen tried unsuccessfully to smother his surprise as his chief continued. "She was, and still is, rather fiery. She practically had other men beating down her door."

"What did you do?"

"I claimed her." Looking at his watch, Jason looked back up to Calen, his wolf shining through his eyes. "I always defend what I claim."

With that, he walked away, leaving Calen to think about that.

CHAPTER FIVE

CHEYENNE

*C*heyenne was on her way to hang out in the kitchen at Lillington's when she'd gotten a text from Ma, the town's fae community coordinator, asking her to pick up the council's notes from their meeting last night from Fire Chief Jason Beckett, the wolf pack's alpha. When Cheyenne stopped by the administration offices, his assistant Lela told her the chief was at the EMS base.

The morning was pleasant, so she'd walked over to the base, enjoying the exercise. She didn't mind that she could still feel the effects of her time with Matt earlier that morning if she moved too much, and she smiled to herself when she saw another ambulance unit pulling out of the bay, raising a brief hand to her in greeting before driving off, heading north on Main street.

"Cheyenne!" one of the medics called when she walked through the doors. He wasn't an alpha, but an all-around nice guy who was fun if he wasn't working on the full moon, Blake Rhodes gave her a friendly smile when she spotted him.

"Blake," she greeted him with an equally friendly expression, walking over for a warm side hug.

"How's it going?" Blake asked.

"Good!"

"Whatcha in for?"

"Oh, I'm looking for the chief. Ma said he had the notes from a meeting she missed last week," Cheyenne explained.

"I think he's back with the Lawsons in the Captain's office," Blake said.

"I'll check, thanks. Catch you later," she said, heading down the hall to the supervisor's office, past the stairs that led to the gym and the apartments kept upstairs for crew members who needed a place to crash after a long shift.

She knocked on the door of the supervisor's office with one knuckle hovering in the doorway. The chief was a handsome man, a silver fox with a powerful frame. As always, Cheyenne's wolf shivered in his presence. Even when he wasn't making an effort to throw around his dominant energy, he just exuded it.

"Cheyenne! Come on in. What can I do for you this morning?" Brian Lawson greeted her cheerfully.

It was probably the knowledge that she was about to get her birth control implant removed today, but even though the full moon was over, she still felt like rubbing herself all over the men who were around. Brian was bisexual and had volunteered to be her donor if she didn't find a mate who was a good fit, and Hazel was ready to make that happen as soon as was socially decent, or before, whichever he consented to.

"I needed the chief, actually."

She looked at her Alpha, nodding respectfully, "Ma said you had the notes from the council meeting last night. She sent me to get them."

"I do. The packet's out in my truck. Just a minute. Have a seat, dear," he instructed, pointing her to a chair.

Brian nodded, and she took a seat.

"Get up to anything fun last night?" Brian asked genially.

"Not really, but I had a delightful morning," she said with a laugh. "I went home with a guy and it was... underwhelming, to say the least."

"I hate it when that happens." Brian shook his head, "You think a guy's the stuff, then he doesn't perform. So, he didn't do it for you, huh?"

"Not at all. It's hard being an alpha female, finding someone who can match my energy and who isn't an alphahole isn't easy." She settled back into the chair. "I just want to stop looking and start a family, you know? I want someone who can be man enough to make me not the man in the relationship, but not at the price of making myself smaller in order to do it."

"Ah, that's hard. I know before Pat and I got together, I went through a lot of alphaholes. I kissed a lot of frogs," Brian said, grimacing at the memory.

"Hey, Brian," Patrick popped his head into the office. "Ryder says that the evaluation for last night's med student is in your inbox, and you may want to look it over before you assign him to a truck today."

"Sure thing."

"Hey Cheyenne, what are you up to today?" Patrick asked, noticing her sitting in the chair. Brian turned away to click on something on his laptop, tsking to himself as he read.

"Oh, just talking about full moon fiascos and kissing frogs," Cheyenne answered with a grin. "It's hard to find a baby daddy when the local alphas are more dud than studs."

Brian looked up from his laptop.

"If you're still thinking you want a baby, Pat and I have been talking about that. If the alpha genetics are important, Patrick said he'd be willing to donate, but if you were looking for a more... intimate donation, then I would be good to help you out. Pat even said he would co-top if you needed his alpha energy to make it the best experience for you." Brian offered her a kind smile. "We'd take good care of you and, of course, we could sit down and talk more about what kind of involvement you'd like."

Patrick nodded his agreement, coming to stand behind Brian, putting a hand on his shoulder and squeezing it briefly.

"Yeah?" Cheyenne looked between the two men. "I'll think about it."

Brian and Patrick were a lovely couple, and if she went with them as fathers, she would have a great set of dads for her baby. Not to mention they were both devastatingly good-looking.

"Come over for dinner. We'll talk more," Patrick invited, stopping when someone appeared in the office's doorway. "I've got a batch of Amish friendship bread going and I need someone to try it out."

"I would love that!" Cheyenne replied with sincere enthusiasm.

"Good. How does Thursday at six-thirty sound? We're both off that night."

"I'll be there," she promised.

Even if she didn't go with Brian and Patrick as the fathers of her child, she wasn't going to pass up an opportunity to enjoy some of Patrick's legendary cooking. Hazel perked up at the idea of being bred by two men like Patrick and Brian, even if Patrick didn't like to actually have sex with women. Cheyenne was just about to ask what she could bring when a familiar voice she didn't want to hear came in through the open office doorway.

CHAPTER SIX

CALEN

"Hey chief, I have a note here to come see you- oh hi." Calen stopped, swallowing hard.

The girl from last night was sitting in the shift supervisor's office, her scent lingering in the small room. She smelled amazing, and Ryne gave an appreciative rumble as Calen stared, at a loss for words.

"He had to grab something from his truck," Brian volunteered, breaking the silence.

"Right. I didn't catch your name last night," Calen said to the girl, who crossed her arms and gave Calen an insincere smile, her eyes narrowed as she looked directly into his eyes.

"I don't remember dropping it," she replied smoothly, eyebrows raising slightly in a challenge his wolf couldn't ignore as she held his gaze and her mouth curved into a smirk. The little minx was taunting him, challenging his wolf.

Her challenge made Ryne wake up and take notice. Calen's lip curled up ever so slightly at her challenge, but she didn't stand to meet him, settling into her seat with apparent ease. She may be challenging him, but he couldn't do anything about it standing in the captain's office, much as he wanted to. She held his gaze, giving him back stare for stare, her haughty expression making his body hum with the desire to subdue her.

He had just decided he didn't care about etiquette, straightening to his full height before he stepped all the way into the office when the chief came back and put a firm, restraining hand on Calen's shoulder.

"Merrick, you need something?" He asked, turning the young man to face him, leveling his gaze, his alpha magic simmering in the bond between them in warning.

Calen narrowed his eyes for a moment, then glanced at Cheyenne and back to his Alpha, mastering himself with visible effort.

"Yeah. I had a question about the parts for 311. It can wait."

"I'll find you when I'm finished here."

"Chief."

Calen left, narrowing his eyes at Cheyenne, who stood to accept the envelope and took a step forward, throwing her shoulders back slightly. Calen clenched his jaw before turning and stomping down the hallway. Cheyenne's smirk faded when the chief turned his gaze to her.

"This is neither the time nor the place for you to be riling him up, understand, young lady?" He reprimanded sternly.

"Yes, alpha. Sorry," she said, dropping her eyes in the face of his show of authority.

"Did you need anything else?"

"No, sir," she replied quietly, taking the yellow packet without meeting his eye, so she missed how he bit back a grin.

"Here you go. Give Ma my compliments."

Cheyenne kept her head tucked, a faint blush of embarrassment at his rebuke staining her cheeks. Brian chuckled as Cheyenne slunk her way out of the office, wiggling her fingers at Brian, but keeping her head down as she followed Calen out.

"Those two are a hoot." Patrick said with a grin, "But damn if it doesn't make me glad I'm not courting anymore."

He set one hand on Brian's shoulder.

"They'd make one hell of a couple if they could sort it out," the chief predicted.

"She'd rip him to shreds," Brian argued. "Besides, from what it sounded like, they spent last night together and it didn't go well."

"Two biological alphas like them, it's usually a battle of wills. I'm going to go see what Merrick needed... besides to get that girl back under him," the chief chuckled.

CHAPTER SEVEN

CHEYENNE

*M*alorie Lillington, known as Ma to anyone but her mate and Jason Beckett, was a boisterous woman, had no children of her own, but had grown up as the middle daughter of eight children, the first seven of which were girls. The Pinehurst wolf pack was so large and unique that things ran a bit differently. Ma ran the diner, Lillington's, that served not only as a place to eat but as a hub for shifters and fae alike.

If you had problems, needed girl time, or just wanted to gossip, you could show up at Ma's kitchen, grab an apron and prep food, or clean. Sage advice, commiseration, and companionship were always served up in the kitchen. That kitchen had seen more than its fair share of broken hearts, bitter exes, moony-eyed lovers, and everything in between.

When Cheyenne had delivered Ma's papers and passed on the chief's respects, she headed straight to the kitchen, where the post-full moon gossip was in full swing, along with the breakfast rush.

"Cheyenne! I saw you left with Calen last night. How was that?" Sophie, one of the wolf shifters who was a little younger than Cheyenne, asked with eager anticipation.

Nineteen and already looking to settle down as seriously as

Cheyenne was, Sophie and Cheyenne often compared notes after the full moon. As a biological alpha female, Cheyenne's tastes ran more dominant than Sophie's. As an omega, Sophie was much more submissive, but they enjoyed sharing notes on their men.

"He's *supposed* to be a biological alpha, but in bed?" Cheyenne shrugged. "I've felt more dominated by my vibrator when I change the batteries out."

"No fireworks?" Sophie asked, eyes wide.

"I faked my orgasms. I met Matt on the way out to my car and went in for a shower at his place."

"You faked them *and* had to double dip? Wow! That's bad. I like Matt though. When we were together, his energy was *so* intense," Sophie said, shivering at the memory. "He's too much for me, but I bet he's right up your alley."

Cheyenne put on her gloves before taking up a block of cheese and a grater. "I just need a guy who's in charge, and a *lot* more dominant."

"Matt's good for that, and if you like it rough…" Lindy, a single fae girl of twenty-two who lived in Red River now, but traveled there for the full moon most months, agreed, giving a chef's kiss above a batch of fresh-baked cinnamon rolls fresh from the oven.

"Yeah, he is. I think I may go back to his place tonight," Cheyenne admitted.

"You should! He's definitely baby daddy material," Sophie said. "He's so nurturing. Every time I see him with the little kids at the pack runs, it makes my ovaries hurt."

"I swear watching him at the June run got me pregnant," one very pregnant girl laughed, rubbing her baby bump affectionately.

"What about you girls? What and who did everyone else get up to?" Cheyenne asked.

"Oh girl," Sophie began. "Let me tell you. Blake Rhodes? The things he can do with his fingers? Pure magic."

"I told you!" Cheyenne said, with a laugh as she grated the cheese into a large container.

Cheyenne spent the morning gossiping and chatting, enjoying the easy camaraderie of Ma's kitchen, some of her tension from the morning easing. She didn't know what it was about Calen this morning, but the way he'd looked at her had set her on edge.

The way he'd looked at her like he was going to grab the back of her neck and bend her over the desk... Cheyenne took a sip of water to cool down the flush in her cheeks at the idea.

Too bad he wasn't more dominant, Hazel thought wistfully. *But then again, did you see that look he gave us in the office? Whew, I thought he was gonna stalk across the office and jerk you around by your ponytail.*

Yeah, what was up with that? Cheyenne said. *Last night he didn't show an ounce of dominance.*

I don't know. Something about him just made me want to challenge him and see what he'd do, Hazel said, tail wagging at the memory of the heat in Calen's eyes as he'd risen to Hazel's challenge.

BY THE TIME Cheyenne left Lillington's, she was in a great mood. She went to her gynecology appointment, had her yearly exam, and had her implant removed without any issues, her doctor assuring her she couldn't wait to see her for midwifery services in a few months.

At lunchtime, she was still so worked up that she'd decided to text Matt when he messaged her.

> **MATT**
> Hey, your legs tired?

> **CHEYENNE**
> Not really, but I've been thinking about this morning all day.

> **MATT**
> Well, you have excellent stamina then, because you've been running through my mind all day.

> **CHEYENNE**
> That was cheesy.

> **MATT**
> I couldn't resist

CHEYENNE

So, I wanted to talk to you about something.
I'm looking for more than just a full moon
tumble.

I really do want a baby, it wasn't just dirty talk.

MATT

Okay.

Is that all you want? Just a baby?

CHEYENNE

No, but I wanted to be super upfront about
that.

MATT

Are you asking me if I'm available for stud
services?

wink emoji

This was what she liked about shifter culture. Humans made things so complicated. Shifters were way more laid-back about sex, mating, and having babies. If a woman just wanted a baby and didn't want to live with a man, it was just as normal as women who wanted to have mates that lived with them.

CHEYENNE

Yeah. If you'd like more, then I would definitely
be willing to explore that too.

MATT

So, this morning was legit…you really want a
baby.

CHEYENNE

Yes.

MATT

I would love to make a baby with you,
Cheyenne. A child would be lucky to have you
as a mother.

Let's have dinner tonight and figure out what
that might look like.

CHEYENNE

I'd love that.

She was in the middle of running another errand when her coworker Shelby had asked her to come in to work the afternoon shift because their driver called in, and their other part-timer was notoriously unavailable the night after the full moon. Cheyenne swung by her apartment, grabbed a uniform shirt, and headed into work.

CHEYENNE HAD BARELY GOTTEN her jacket off when Shelby rushed out the front door to the already-loaded delivery van, calling over her shoulder that five orders had come through since she'd called. Cheyenne switched the radio from the country music that Shelby preferred to the classic rock and roll that Cheyenne kept on in the background and got to work.

Cheyenne worked steadily through the afternoon cutting fruit and then making chocolate-dipped strawberries, pineapple, and banana slices. She even separated an orange into segments, dipping them in chocolate for a lunch replacement.

When Ben dropped by with a thank-you lunch for her and Shelby, Cheyenne was cleaning up the chocolate station.

"Good work today, girls," the older man said, running a finger through his salt-and-pepper hair. "I know it was your day off Cheyenne, thank you for coming in."

"It's no problem," Cheyenne assured.

It was always busy the night after the full moon, so she wasn't surprised when the front door chimed. Shelby went up front as Cheyenne drizzled white chocolate artfully over milk chocolate-dipped strawberries.

"Hey Shelby, is Cheyenne in?" a man's voice asked. Ben looked up and wiggled his eyebrows, offering her a grin.

"Yeah, she's in the back. Let me get her," Shelby said.

"Matt is out front for you." Shelby wiggled her eyebrows much in the same manner Ben had a moment before.

"Really?" She wasn't supposed to see him till tonight.

Her chest tightened. She hoped he wasn't canceling and hadn't rethought having a baby. She steeled herself, reminding herself that it was okay if Matt didn't want this, and that she could still go with Patrick and Brian. Hazel suggested that any of these options would be good.

"I'll finish those. Go see what he wants," Shelby offered, snapping her own gloves on, elbowing Cheyenne gently with an encouraging smile.

Peeling off her gloves, Cheyenne patted her hair.

"You look hot," Shelby assured her. Straightening her shirt, Cheyenne walked out to the lobby.

"Good afternoon," he said a little formally.

"Hi," she replied, with a confused smile as she wondered what he was doing there.

"I'm sorry to bother you at work. I'm sure you're busy," he swallowed and offered her a charming smile.

"We're not too busy now. What's up?"

"My wolf wouldn't leave me alone after we talked. I wanted to clarify something about what we discussed this morning."

"Um, okay." She shoved her hands in her pockets, her anxious thoughts spinning.

Great, he was rethinking it. No big deal, she could always go talk to Brian and Patrick. They would make amazing dads. It wasn't exactly what she wanted, but she could always find her mate later.

"I know I'm putting you on the spot, and I apologize for that. But while you're looking for more than just a baby daddy, I would like to be at the top of your list of mates to consider."

He stepped to the side of the counter where she stood, his eyes dark with desire and firm determination.

"Oh." Her wolf preened and Cheyenne took a deep breath.

I mean... he's a nice man, Hazel conceded.

He stared into her eyes as he stalked toward her, reaching for her hand, tugging it gently out of her pocket to take it in his.

"You want more, for sure?" She asked, eyes going wide.

"With you, yes," he confirmed.

"Well. I hadn't really talked to anyone else seriously yet," she admitted.

"So, I'm the whole list?" He asked, looking supremely satisfied. "Good. I like that. Tonight, I'd like to give you a reason to keep it that way."

He took her hand, kissing the inside of her wrist, nipping gently with his teeth.

"I'll see you tonight," he said with a wink before releasing her hand.

"Yeah, sounds good."

Walking back into the kitchen, Ben was sipping his coffee with an enormous grin, while Shelby looked like she was ready to swoon.

"Oh, my magic!" Shelby squealed while Cheyenne flushed with pleasure.

"Well that was - unexpected," Cheyenne admitted, taking the tray of finished chocolate strawberries to the cooler.

"He wants to be the whole list," Shelby quoted dreamily. "I don't know about you, but my panties evaporated when he said that."

"Yeah, mine too."

Cheyenne took care to set the strawberries in the section of the walk-in cooler right in front of the fan to help the chocolate harden faster.

"If you don't jump on that, send him my way. 'I want to be at the top of the list' indeed. He made it to the top of my list!" Shelby crowed.

"You're not even looking for a mate, are you?" Ben asked.

"I might be if he's available!" Shelby said, popping a piece of pineapple into her mouth from the scraps they were turning into fruit salad.

"Well, I guess I'll let you know." Cheyenne laughed. "But I have a feeling that he's going to be a great fit."

"So, tell me what your ideal life looks like," Matt said later that night over dinner.

He'd listened while she described what she wanted: a small family with a strong male partner to lead her. He'd asked a slew of thoughtful questions, then walked her to her door respectfully at the end of the evening.

"I don't know that I'm entirely what you're looking for," he said honestly, "But I'd like to give this a try with you. I want to give you everything you want, and if that means I'm here to give you a baby and then I'm here to hold space for you to have the right bonded mate for you down the road, I'm okay with that."

"Really?"

This sounded too good to be true. It was, right? There was no way that this good-looking man who loved kids and rocked her world in the bedroom was willing to be her baby daddy and be open to more. This was exactly what she wanted.

Maybe she didn't *need* an alpha. Maybe a strong beta male was enough for her.

Hazel grumbled but admitted grudgingly that Matt was pretty great, even though he wasn't an alpha.

"Yes. I know that you're an alpha and you're probably looking for someone to stand on a more equal footing. I don't know that I'm as dominant as you want outside of the bedroom, but I really enjoy you. As far as women I like, I would love to have a baby with you. We're already friends, and I'll take good care of you, during a pregnancy and after."

Cheyenne smiled and took a bite of her food, chewing slowly as she considered.

"Are you sure?"

"Yeah. I've been thinking about having kids for a little bit, and I was going to add my name to the list of guys looking for a mate, but I just hadn't done it yet."

Cheyenne was trying to think of a suitable reply to that when he took a deep breath and took a step closer.

"Yes. I've got an early morning, so let me do this," he took the bag of leftovers from her hand, set it down at her feet, then pushed her against her front door.

He held her gaze for just a moment before pressing his lips to hers in a firm kiss, his hand snaking up her neck, his fingers sliding beneath her hair as he claimed her mouth.

When he withdrew, he winked and picked up her bag of food, handing it to her.

"Now, get inside. Can't have my future baby mama getting chilly."

"Thanks for an amazing night," she began, but he shook his head and made a twirling motion with his finger.

"Mm-mm, inside, ma'am." He placed his hands on her shoulders, spun her around to face her front door, and swatted her bottom playfully. "You can text me that mushy stuff when you're inside where it's warm. My phone's not going anywhere."

As she put her leftovers away, she was thrilled with how things had developed. The date night with Calen might not have ended up how she wanted, but it certainly wasn't going to turn her nose up at how today had gone. She really liked Matt, and also, she appreciated his open-minded approach.

She wasn't sure he was as assertive as she wanted her lifetime bonded mate to be, but it seemed like they were a good fit for now. He certainly seemed like a good guy to have around in the perimeter of her child's life.

Things were definitely looking up for her.

CHAPTER EIGHT

CALEN

"Okay, I'll be back Thursday after those parts come in," Calen said on his way out the door at the end of his shift.

"See you then. Thanks for your work today," the chief said without looking up from the paperwork in his hands.

"Sir?" Calen said, hesitating.

"Hm?"

"What was the name of that girl - the one in your office this morning?" Calen asked.

The chief looked up, folding the top edge of his paperwork down, glaring at Calen over its edge.

"If you didn't bother to learn her name before you took her home, I'm not telling you, son," the Alpha informed him with a disapproving scowl.

Calen wanted to say something defensive back but held his tongue.

"Yes, sir," Calen said, biting back a sharp reply.

The old man had clearly forgotten what it was like on the full moon when you were young and unmated. Some things, like names, were just not important in the heat of the moment. She certainly hadn't asked for his either. She'd initiated things with him, anyway, it wasn't like he was the insensitive, uncaring one. She hadn't even stayed for breakfast after.

You sound like a whiny bitch, Ryne commented.

Fuck you, Ryne, Calen shot back.

Calen wasn't a jerk for not asking for her name when she hadn't so much as asked for his before following him back to his place and falling into bed with him.

Stomping out the front door, he shook his head and decided to go for a run to clear his head before heading home. Maybe getting up in the mountains and letting his wolf roam wasn't such a bad idea for getting his mind off the girl.

CHAPTER NINE

CHEYENNE

*B*rian opened the front door, gesturing her inside, the scent of freshly baked bread and some other savory dish that smelled divine wafting out tantalizingly.

"This is for you," she said, holding up the bottle of wine.

"I said you didn't need to bring anything," Brian said with a slight frown, but took the bottle of wine from her, taking her hand and planting a kiss on the backs of her fingers.

She blushed and allowed him to place her hand back at her side.

"Come on in. Pat's still fussing over dinner, would you like a drink?"

"I am not *fussing*, you uncultured Neanderthal! Presentation is important!" Patrick called from the kitchen.

"I would love one," Cheyenne said, grinning.

"What would you like? I can open this if you prefer, or we've got just about anything you could want."

"Wine would be lovely," Cheyenne said, slipping out of her jacket.

"Alright, I'll take that and come back with a glass. Make yourself comfortable."

Brian left with her jacket slung over his arm and Cheyenne looked around the room, Patrick was always adding and changing things about their decor, making every visit to their home a new opportunity to enjoy different art.

The television had been replaced with an enormous abstract painting that reminded Cheyenne of pink drops of paint on a white canvas. It hung over the mantle, dominating the space. She noted it, wanting to say something to Patrick. Another painting hung on one wall depicting a mountain scene that looked similar to one of the well-known peaks near Pinehurst.

"Here you go," Brian said from behind her.

Thanking him for the wine, she took it and had a sip.

"So, tell me," Brian began, but Patrick's voice came from the kitchen.

"Dinner is ready!"

Brian rolled his eyes and flashed her a long-suffering grin.

"I asked him if it was ready when I was in there and he said no," Brian informed her with a chuckle.

"It wasn't ready then," Patrick said, standing in the doorway of the kitchen holding a stack of plates, one hand resting on his hip, throwing his mate a roll of his eyes. "The garnish wasn't on yet!"

While Patrick described everything from their steaks and mushrooms with some delicious sauce to the potatoes and the macaroni that Patrick had made with some cheese, then lastly the artisan sourdough bread he'd pulled from the oven and sliced while Cheyenne and Brian helped themselves to the rest of dinner.

"I can do that, honey," Brian said, eying his mate.

"And touch my bread? As if," Patrick said with a sniff. "You get your food and don't forget to leave room for the Amish friendship bread for dessert. It's earl grey with a to-die-for earl grey icing.

"I saw your new art in the living room! I really like the new paintings especially," she said.

Pat gave Brian a look Cheyenne didn't understand and thanked her, but Brian changed the subject hastily.

"So, tell us about this guy who's caught your eye," Brian said, grinning.

Cheyenne hedged. They hadn't talked about if they were telling people just yet, and she didn't want to out Matt to his bosses if he didn't want that.

"Actually, I need to use your restroom really quick," she said.

"Sure thing, you know where it is," Patrick said easily.

> **CHEYENNE**
>
> Hey, so I have a question.

MATT

Alright.

> **CHEYENNE**
>
> Um, I don't want to come off as clingy or weird. Whatever your answer is, it's fine, okay?

MATT

Cheyenne, sweetie, my tongue was inside of your pussy this morning. I can handle a question.

Whatcha got?

> **CHEYENNE**
>
> Are we... telling people? About us?

MATT

Sure

> **CHEYENNE**
>
> Sure, like you want to? Or sure like it's fine?

MATT

Um, I don't know what that means. Yes, tell people. Tell everyone you know. Put it on social media. Hell, rent a billboard if you want.

I'm thrilled to be your prospective mate, babe.

Just got a call, gotta run.

Cheyenne took care of her business and reemerged in the dining room.

"I told you people would like the painting," Patrick was saying. "You should be proud of it!"

"I *am* proud of it," Brian replied in an irritated whisper. "That doesn't mean I need it hanging up in the living room where people will see it."

"Mm-hmm," Patrick said.

Cheyenne smothered a smile as she walked back into the dining room.

"So, dish," Brian instructed.

"Well, you know Matt Griffith? I think he's on Black shift, not one of your guys," she said, looking between the two EMS Captains.

"Oooooh. He's nice-looking. Not my type, obviously," Brian gave an affectionate look to his mate, who rolled his eyes.

Patrick and Brian both looked like their genetics were a mix between a brick house and a football linebacker, but Patrick was a power-lifter with a massive broad, powerful frame with sandy hair that was long on top, enough to fall into his eyes as he worked. Brian's build was the same as Patrick's, but, as Brian told it, he wasn't allowed to be any more trim than he was, so he could be the designated bread tester for his husband, and bread testers couldn't look like statues of Greek gods.

"Well, he's the guy I was with after Calen and I hooked up on the last full moon," she explained.

"Nice choice," Brian nodded his approval.

Cheyenne explained about Matt's offer, and how he wanted to be at the top of the list of her prospective mates.

"Oh, how romantic," Brian sighed, looking at Patrick with dreamy eyes.

"Very romantic," Patrick said gruffly. "Eat your food before it gets cold."

They finished their dinner, with Brian and Patrick wishing her all the best, Patrick sending her home with enough leftovers to feed her and Shelby lunch for at least two days.

CHEYENNE

Hey, handsome.

45

MATT

Well, hello yourself, beautiful.

CHEYENNE

If you're not too tired, you're welcome to come over tonight.

MATT

I don't know how energetic I'll be. I'm likely to fall asleep. We had five calls overnight.

CHEYENNE

You can come and sleep here if you want.

MATT

That sounds better than you know, but I'm afraid I'm going to be useless to you unless you're looking to use me while I lay there.

CHEYENNE

I was thinking we could just…sleep.

MATT

That sounds perfect.

Oh, how was dinner with the Lawson's?

CHEYENNE

It was nice, but how about we talk about it tomorrow when you're not exhausted?

MATT

I think that might be the sexiest thing I've ever heard a woman say.

See you when I'm off.

Cheyenne smiled at her phone and told him to come on in when he got there. In less than ten minutes she was home, the leftovers put away, and she jumped in a quick shower. She heard Matt call out when he came in, but by the time she got out into the bedroom, he was asleep on the bed, on top of the covers, phone in hand.

She took it gently and plugged it in, setting it on the nightstand.

She glanced at the screen, where an unfinished text message was open.

MATT

Hey babe, I'll probably be asleep by the time you're out of the shower, just wanted to say thank you forrrrr

Cheyenne smiled and covered him with a blanket. Clearly he'd fallen asleep mid-text. Hazel conceded and said he was a nice enough boy, for now.

CHAPTER TEN

CALEN

*I*t took him a little over three weeks to find her. During those twenty-four days, he'd spent an inordinate amount of his time wondering how a woman as beautiful as she was stayed out of his notice in a small town like Pinehurst.

He was so desperate to find her, he'd even volunteered to be the medic on standby for the high school wrestling team. He had no reason to think she would be there, but it just pissed him off to sit at home and think about her, so he figured he might as well get out and get some overtime.

He'd created several versions of the speech he wanted to deliver that would convince her to give him another try.

You're as bad as Xander and Ryder, his wolf chided. *It's a good thing I have more self-control than Xander or we'd be a laughingstock, being the next ones imprinted.*

Calen grimaced and went to retort, but he spotted her and the moment he caught sight of her smile, all the words fled from his mind. She was under Matt Griffith's arm. Her head leaned on Matt's shoulder as she looked at something he had pulled up on his phone. It was all Calen could do to wait until the light turned and traffic had cleared enough on Main Street so he could cross into the diner he'd watched them walk into together, hand in hand.

By the time he got into the diner, they were sitting side by side in a booth, her hand under the table resting on - well, it better only be his thigh, Calen thought, his wolf growling at the idea.

"What are you thinking?" She asked Matt.

"It isn't decent to say," Matt answered, looking at her slyly out of the corner of his eye with a grin that sent Calen's blood pressure through the roof.

"About the *menu*! What are you ordering *off the menu?*" She leaned into him, poking his ribs.

Matt snorted and grabbed her hand, giving her a chuckle.

"Probably the steak. What about you?"

"I'm thinking about the fried onion petal burger, but the steak looks good, too."

She peeked at Matt through her lashes. Shifter culture had changed in the modern world. While it was acceptable for a man to buy a woman dinner casually, like a human date, sharing food implied a relationship. Wolves brought food to their mates, so sharing their own food was a signal from a potential mate - a promise to provide for them.

"If you want to split our meals, we could do that," Matt said, sliding an arm around her shoulder and pressing a kiss to the side of her forehead.

Calen didn't wait for her to answer; *that* was not going to fucking happen. Strolling over to their table, he asked without preamble or a polite introduction, lacing his voice with all of his alpha magic and authority.

"Have you claimed this female?"

"I have not," Matt said, speaking slowly.

"Yield," Calen said, loudly enough that the other tables in the diner went quiet, but didn't let his wolf lace it with authority.

Matt raised an eyebrow, but leaned back in the bench seat, readjusting his arm around Calen's girl's shoulders.

"No."

Ryne, always waiting just below the surface, ready to grasp the authority that he perceived as his right, tried to force Calen to shift and take this upstart beta down a peg. He might not be crazy about the girl, but his human was, and that was enough for Ryne. Regardless of the issue of the female, there was no way he was letting some beta challenge them and let it go.

"Yield or fight," Calen's voice rang with all the authority of an alpha.

It was dangerous territory for a biological alpha to stake a claim of any kind. Claiming a mate, using your position as an alpha implied a level of power and authority over a member of the pack that he didn't technically have. He would have to go before the council and ask the Alpha to uphold it, but that was something he could deal with later.

"Seriously, Calen?" Matt asked with a sigh, his jaw ticking. "I don't want to do this with you. I just want to eat my dinner and go home with my girl."

Calen's jaw ticked at Matt's insinuation that Calen's girl belonged to him, and he nearly lost it when Cheyenne hadn't corrected him, or looked phased by it at all.

"I'll have Ma make you a doggie bag," Calen said with a smirk, supremely confident in his ability to take Matt in a fight.

"You know what? Fine." Matt said, sliding out of the booth slowly. Cheyenne looked between both men with a little frown but didn't try to stop them. Matt slipped out of his jacket and handed it back to her with a wink. "Hold this for me, babe?"

"Sure," she said, sighing in resignation.

Matt led the way. Calen followed him outside, shedding his own jacket as they walked out the back door. He draped it over a milk crate.

"She doesn't want to date you, much less be your mate, man," Matt said, stepping backwards as Calen rolled his shoulders. "So what's the point?"

"I want her."

"She doesn't want you."

"She doesn't know me."

"She knows enough. Seriously, this is the dumbest thing," Matt said. Calen wasn't listening. The back door of the diner swung open, and his girl came out with her arms crossed over her chest, eyes blazing. The look in her eyes turned his resolve to steel. He was going to fucking have her.

"Skin or fur?" Calen asked, dragging his eyes reluctantly from Cheyenne.

"Skin," Matt answered.

Calen nodded and stepped in with a solid swing that sent Matt staggering backwards. Calen pursued with a ferocity that caught Matt off guard. The fight was over when Calen grabbed Matt by the front of the shirt, throwing him into the dumpster with a resounding gong that echoed off the back wall of the diner. Matt slumped to the ground, head lolling. Calen walked forward to check on him, lifting his head. Matt groaned and knocked his hand away.

"Fucker," Matt growled.

"You yield?" Calen asked.

"Matt, it's okay," Cheyenne said from behind Calen. "There's no point in you beating each other to hell over this. Call it."

"No," Matt growled, grimacing as he tried to stand, putting a hand to his ribs.

She stepped in between the two of them, ignoring Calen.

"Seriously, I don't want you to do this," she said, putting her hands on his chest.

"Fine." Matt said, then looked at Calen over her shoulder, "I yield. You can try to claim her. Good luck, considering you couldn't keep her happy for one full moon."

Matt kissed her on the cheek, ignoring a threatening growl from Calen. His girl slipped off the jacket and returned it to Matt. He took it with his lips pursed.

"Call me later?" He couldn't call her without directly challenging Calen, but there was nothing stopping her from calling anyone she wanted if she hadn't accepted Calen's claim.

"Yeah, I will," she promised.

Matt headed back inside without a word, shaking his head. The moment the door shut behind Matt, his girl whirled around to face him, her face a mask of sharp irritation.

"What the hell? No one claims people anymore. That's not even a thing. I have zero interest in you, Calen." He still didn't know her name, but that didn't matter.

The blaze of defiance in her eyes was turning him on, and awakening the alpha inside of him. When he didn't respond, she turned on her heel and stormed back into the restaurant. He took a minute to spit the blood from his mouth, then followed her inside. She'd moved to the other side of the table and perched on the very edge of her seat. He took Matt's place smoothly, removing his jacket.

"We can still split the steak if you like."

The waiter brought her a large frozen alcoholic drink from the bar. She sipped it irritably.

"What are you drinking?"

"An Adios Motherfucker," she informed him.

"Ironic."

"Funny, I was just thinking the same thing," she replied.

His wolf grumbled. *I don't understand why we need this one. She's... grumpy.*

I want this one, Calen insisted.

Fine, Ryne sighed. *If you'd rather have a girl with a temper like fireworks instead of a nice girl who, I don't know, you know, wants us, that's your choice.*

"Are you two ready to order?" The waiter asked.

"I think I'll just have my drink and go. He'll be paying," she nodded toward Calen, who nodded in return and pulled out his wallet, throwing it down on the table and taking a seat across the table from her.

You're right, Calen mused. *She's like a firecracker. I like that.*

An unenthusiastic *ugh* was Ryne's only reply.

"She'll have the onion petal burger, petals on the side, and I'll have the 22-ounce steak with a baked potato," Calen ordered smugly.

He had no illusions about how this night would go. She was an alpha female, and he'd just crashed her date with a potential mate that she really liked. As mad as she was, though, her arousal when she'd been with Matt had been nothing compared to when Calen had nearly knocked Matt out. She was so aroused right now he bet every shifter in the place could smell her.

Yes, she was pissed, but he was confident she would come around. She would take some time to come around to his way of thinking, but they were going to work it out.

"What's in your drink?"

"Want a taste?" She offered, her eyes glinting mischievously.

"Only if you're willing to share with me," he teased.

She took another sip, then nodded, leaning forward across the table. Surprised, he leaned forward to sip from her glass. She flicked her wrist, sending the concoction into his face.

"Damn it!"

Firecracker, indeed, Ryne thought with a dry chuckle.

Shut up, Calen snapped at his wolf.

"Sorry about the mess," their woman said to the waiter, who stood staring at them from a few tables away, then she walked out.

Calen was cursing, standing to follow her, and said shortly to the waiter, "Make my order a carry-out order for 9 o'clock."

"We close at 9 on weekdays."

"For 8:30 then," Calen snapped.

"You got it."

Calen took off after her, still cursing as he wiped the burning alcohol from his eyes. He caught up with her easily enough.

"Where are you going?"

"To see the chief," she responded lightly.

"He'll be eating dinner," Calen said, regarding her uneasily.

There were two things you never did in the Pinehurst pack: interrupt the chief's dinner for anything other than a life or death emergency where his presence would save the person in question, or disrespect his mate, Miss Linda.

They walked silently along Main Street. He stopped her before she opened the front gate with a hand on one of the whitewashed wooden planks.

"Hey, what's your name?" Calen asked casually.

"Are you serious right now?" She demanded, her face a mask of indignation.

"As a heart attack," he said, offering her a cocky grin.

"You spent the night with me, tried to make some bullshit claim on me, and you don't even know my name? Un-fucking-believable!" She opened the gate and walked in, shaking her head.

CHAPTER ELEVEN

FIRE CHIEF JASON BECKETT, PINEHURST PACK ALPHA

"We might have company for dinner," Jason said, a thoughtful, distant look on his face. His mate didn't turn around or ask him how he knew, just looked around her kitchen considering the dinner she'd prepared.

"How many?"

"Two: a male and female, both alphas."

"Alright, let me throw together some dessert, then," she said, biting the inside of her cheek for a moment before moving into action.

"I was thinking about our courtship today," he mused, watching her work, admiring the lines of her body.

"Were you? What brought that up?" Linda asked without looking up from her work at the counter.

"You know Calen?"

"Hm," she said thoughtfully as she stirred the vegetables on the stove, pursing her lips in thought. "Remind me which one he is?"

"Biological alpha, does truck maintenance at the base. Calen Merrick."

"Oh, he's a nice boy."

"Mmhmm. Reminds me a lot of me."

That got her attention, and she glanced up from her cooking.

"Does he? Are you thinking he may be a good fit to be the next alpha?"

"I'm considering it. I want to see how this thing pans out with a girl he's pursuing," he said, taking a sip of his drink as he chuckled, remembering the chemistry between the two young people in the office a few weeks back. The boy had been distracted and on edge ever since.

"Jason Beckett, did you plant ideas in his head about your backwards notion of courtship?" Linda demanded, whirling to wave her spatula threateningly. He narrowed his eyes, but she didn't back down, glaring at him.

"A young alpha came to me with a problem. I shared my life experiences as a teaching aid." He raised an eyebrow, standing to his full height.

Completely unperturbed, his mate glared up at him, placing her hands on her hips. Her eyes went from dark brown to blue as her wolf made its presence known, her mouth set into a determined line.

"You are impossible! I can't believe-" she started to rebuke as he came around the island slowly, his eyes narrowed as his wolf grinned at the idea of making their mate submit to them. She backed away, brandishing her spatula. "Don't you look at me like that! I have dinner to make and we have guests coming. I don't need your distracting shenanigans right now!"

Jason's wolf rose fully to the forefront of his mind, pushing aside human niceties.

"Mate, I'm alpha in this house and I expect to be shown the respect I'm due," Jason said, his own wolf yipping in pleasure at the idea of distracting their mate in the best way.

"Don't you pull that alpha nonsense on me. You may be an alpha out there, but this is *my* kitchen."

"I am in charge in every room of this house," he retorted, hackles rising.

"You're in charge in *every* room in this house, are you? Well fine. Here." Linda took off her apron, throwing it at his chest, shoving the spatula into his hands, turning off the egg timer for the chicken in the oven.

"Linda," he said in a conciliatory tone, his wolf shrinking at his mate's wrath, leaving Jason to pick up the pieces of the mess he'd created. His wolf would rather face a room full of psychotic gunmen than deal with their mate in a temper.

"Oh no, *Mr. Alpha*, you're in charge in here, which makes you and all your big alpha energy in charge of dinner. I'll make myself a drink, prop my feet up and take it easy," she announced, grabbing a two glasses from the cabinet.

"That isn't what I meant."

"Oh no, I would hate to not give you the respect you're due, *alpha*. I'll get out of your way."

"Linda…" he pleaded, then fell silent when she didn't deign to respond. Jason's wolf receded, lapsing into total silence.

She grabbed a bottle of wine out of the fridge, heading for the covered porch.

Grumbling, he opened the door and called out, "How much longer does the chicken bake?"

"I don't know, I'm not in charge!" She called back over her shoulder.

He considered going after her, but twenty-four years of marriage teaches a man things. First, there was no way she was cooking dinner. He could order her around until he was blue in the face, but once she dug her heels in, she was as stubborn as he was.

Second, as much as he hated to admit it, she was right. They'd come to an agreement many years before about authority in the kitchen. Her domain was absolute. As an alpha herself, she was responsible for the pack the same way in her own unique way, but she needed a space that she ruled over. This was her den, much like his office.

He'd gotten worked up and overreacted, and cooking them dinner was the beginning of how he would make it up to her. The knowledge that he was in the wrong didn't make his situation any more pleasant, and it didn't change the fact that he couldn't cook his way out of a cardboard box, or that they'd remodeled the kitchen last year and he still didn't understand how the fancy oven with its knobs and buttons worked.

Linda saw the approaching couple stop at the gate, then an angry girl stormed in.

"Cheyenne, lovely to see you!" Linda greeted.

"Miss Linda, I hope I'm not interrupting," Cheyenne approached, giving a furtive glance at the young male trailing behind her, who looked pleased at something Linda didn't understand.

"No, dear. Come sit down," Linda invited, holding up a glass of wine in invitation to Cheyenne, who nodded and went to sit in the rocking chair closest to the front door.

"Oh no, not there. That's Jason's spot. Come sit on the swing with me," Linda invited with a tilt of her head. Cheyenne nodded, steering away from the matching rocker, built somewhat larger than Linda's, heading to the porch swing.

"What brings you here?" Linda asked, noting how the young man she now recognized stood awkwardly, his hands shoved into his pockets.

"That would be me, ma'am. I have a pressing need to see the Alpha," Calen said.

"Goodness, what did you do to yourself?" Lind asked, observing his swollen lip, sticky wet shirt, and disreputable hair.

"A spilled drink," he explained shortly, pressing his lips together.

Linda smiled, accepting the story without comment, suspecting that the woman sitting beside him may have "spilled" it onto his face.

"Go around to the kitchen, dear. Let yourself in. No need to knock."

"Yes, ma'am."

"Wine?" Lind asked when Calen had rounded the corner.

"Yes, please."

"Now, I want to chat, but I need to make a quick call."

Linda picked up her phone, dialing the number she knew by heart.

"Pete, it's Linda. Can you have someone run us over three large meat lovers pizzas, an order of cheese sticks, and two lava cakes? You're a doll. Charge it to my husband's account."

She hung up the phone and looked over at the younger girl with a kind smile, pouring them two glasses of wine.

"Now, tell me what you're here about."

CHAPTER TWELVE

CALEN

"Chief?" Calen said, entering the kitchen without knocking, but hovering just inside the doorway as a wave of energy hit Calen, rough and irritated.

"*What?*" His alpha snapped at Calen's intrusion.

"Miss Linda sent me in," Calen began.

"Oh, great. Stir that."

He handed Calen a slotted spoon, nodding to a pot on the stove that was boiling with enthusiasm.

"Sir, I don't think you're supposed to boil them like this," Calen said, looking at the contents of the pan dubiously.

"Then fix it," his alpha snapped.

A timer beeped for the chicken. Jason turned and opened the oven door and checked it, but shook his head, sticking it back in. He closed the oven and looked over the kitchen in dismay, running his fingers through disheveled hair that stuck up at odd angles.

"What do you want, Merrick?" Jason asked, glancing at Calen as if he'd just realized he wasn't there to help him save this disaster of a dinner.

"Well, sir, I came to get your approval for something."

Calen switched off the burner and set aside the overcooked green beans.

"What's that?"

"I...claimed a girl," Calen explained.

"You claimed her?" Jason turned, the flowery apron that stretched over his uniform shirt looking absurd stretched over his massive frame, but doing nothing to dim the alpha energy rolling off him in waves now.

"Yes, sir."

"A local girl? From my pack?" The dangerous glint in his eye made Calen want to retreat, but he stood straighter, pushing his shoulders back, and lifted his chin.

You know, now would be the perfect time to apologize and back out of this whole thing, Ryne suggested.

You know, you could be helpful, Calen replied acidly.

You're really committed to this? Ryne asked, sighing mentally.

Yes. Obviously, or I wouldn't be here.

I don't understand why, Ryne said, but Calen felt his energy rise to meet the chief's square on in a show of solidarity with Calen's desire.

"Yes," Calen said, lacing his voice with his own alpha energy, his eyes meeting the older man's with no hesitation.

"For mating," his alpha said, narrowing his eyes.

"Yes," Calen said.

Thank you, Calen said to Ryne.

Mm-hmm, Ryne grumbled.

"What does *she* have to say about it?" the Chief asked.

"She threw a drink in my face," Calen admitted with a grimace.

The Chief's dark look receded and transformed to one of amusement. He chuckled and nodded. Calen looked up in surprise. The older man's mood had lightened considerably.

"Sounds about right. So - what are your plans?" He looked at the bread in the bottom oven, scowling at it and examining it with a dubious expression.

"To court her?" Calen replied, confused.

"Outside of that. Do you want to be the leader of this pack?"

"Alpha, I have no intention of challenging your authority."

"And yet, here you are, informing me you've done just that," the older man's voice held no threat, but a slight shift in his energy put Calen and Ryne back on edge.

"I have no intention of challenging your authority over ruling the pack. If you see my claim as a problem, I will withdraw from the territory as soon as I've claimed my mate," Calen said, his heart sinking at the idea.

Leaving Pinehurst was the last thing Calen wanted, but seeing Cheyenne tonight made him realize she was the girl he wanted for his mate. In his mind, Ryne gave a loud growl of displeasure at the idea.

"Should bread look like this? Is it supposed to be that dark?"

"I don't make bread, chief. Maybe we should call Miss Linda and ask her," Calen said, giving the bread an uneasy look.

"You're some help." Jason removed the bread from the oven, pressing his lips together for a moment before dumping it out onto the counter and muttering to himself. "Yeah. That looks good, I think."

The chief nodded in satisfaction, grinning at the bread, then turned his sharp gaze back on Calen.

"I won't stand in the way of your claim, but you're going to help me finish this dinner."

TWENTY-FIVE MINUTES LATER, the ladies were enjoying lava cakes and wine on the porch when both men emerged, looking frazzled.

"Linda, I- oh. I love you," the alpha sighed, spotting the pizza boxes and offering her a sheepish smile.

"There are plates in the bag," Miss Linda informed him primly, nodding to the bag that rested on top of the pizza boxes.

Jason knelt before his mate, taking her hand with tender affection, and, turning it over, he placed a delicate kiss on the inside of her wrist and gave it a little love bite. Linda sniffed but didn't pull back and Ryne made an amused noise as he and Calen realized she was playing hard to get with the chief and making him pay for some infraction he'd committed.

"I apologize, mama," the Chief said in a quiet, humble undertone that was more suitable to the bedroom than the front porch with company only a few feet away.

Calen looked away, not wanting to intrude on what suddenly felt like a private moment.

"Mm-hmm. And what state is my kitchen in, Mr. Beckett?"

With a sheepish grin, the Chief admitted, "Abysmal." Then, without looking at Calen, he said, "Calen volunteered to clean it up."

Calen's head snapped up, his mouth opening, then shutting like a goldfish. Cheyenne snickered, biting her lip as her eyes dropped to her pizza. He offered her a glare.

If you'd picked a decent mate, she might offer to help you with that, you know, Ryne pointed out.

You know what? I hear you don't get it, but also, can you just go along with this, please?

Gods, you haven't imprinted, have you? Ryne asked, alarmed at the thought. *I think I would know, wouldn't I? Ew. I hope not. You could do better.*

I haven't imprinted, dipshit, Calen said, not quite managing to suppress a roll of his eyes. *Also, don't talk about her like that. She's great.*

I'm just checking! Ryne said. *It would explain why you're so determined about someone so ordinary, and a little hostile to our efforts.*

Ryne, Calen growled.

Alright, alright, I'll be supportive, even though this is stupid. There are plenty of girls who are, you know... interested.

I want her, Calen thought back.

"How sweet of Calen," Linda said, not taking her eyes off her mate.

"Yes ma'am."

Calen grabbed a few slices of pizza and took the only available seat beside Cheyenne on the porch swing. She'd scooted so far to the side that the armrest dug into her hip after a few minutes, which made him want to snatch her back and pull her onto his lap, but he refrained. The group chatted with ease, on the older couple's part with a minimal strain of awkwardness about the weather and the upcoming full moon festival, while Cheyenne watched the alpha and his mate with a wistful expression.

The tender way the Chief spoke to his mate, the way he refilled her wine glass and the way he took her hand almost tentatively, how he drew her onto his lap, and the way he whispered into her ear until a delicate blush rose to her cheeks, just then he didn't look like an Alpha. Calen's alpha looked like any other male courting and flattering his mate after a fight, earning his way back into her good graces.

Calen watched Cheyenne and took notes about the things that made her face soften until she caught him looking and fixed her face to reveal less of her thoughts.

"Well, it's been a lovely evening. Calen, Cheyenne, feel free to take some pizza home. I have business with my mate. Calen, don't forget the kitchen."

Cheyenne rose to go, Calen sighed but didn't argue, watching her wistfully. He didn't want to end the evening here. He wanted to see her home, as was proper for the first date.

"Oh, Cheyenne dear, stay and let him walk you back home. I couldn't bear it if something happened to you," Linda said, smiling with saccharine sweetness.

Cheyenne was about to object when she saw Jason raise his eyebrows at her as he tilted his head to be seen around Linda's shoulder, she understood this was not a request. Cheyenne nodded and Calen smirked in satisfaction. She would at least have to let him walk her home now.

"Sure thing. I'll get started on the cleaning," Cheyenne said, standing off the porch swing.

Calen wasted no time following her to the kitchen. She went straight to the sink, got rid of the ruined food, and started on the dishes. Calen didn't make any comments, helping with muted efficiency, trying to stay out of her way and avoiding pissing her off, while still being helpful.

When banging noises echoed through the house and noises of an unmistakable and intimate nature could be heard in the kitchen, making both of them blush, Calen started chatting to cover the noise.

"He's an amazing leader, but man couldn't cook to save his life. He was boiling these vegetables to mush," Calen commented as the sound of footsteps running through the house, then heavier ones following close behind, and a feminine shriek sounded through the house.

"The bread was worse," Cheyenne said, eyeing the loaves. The outside was a stunning golden brown, but the inside had been raw, uncooked dough when Jason cut it. After that, the Chief had taken off his mate's apron and announced that he was going to go apologize to Miss Linda, his expression grim.

"You should have seen him. He was so proud until he cut into it. I thought he was going to throw it, and it looked like he thought about it, but I bet Miss Linda would have jerked a knot in his tail for that," Calen chuckled.

"They're funny," she admitted, blushing when a thud and a creaking of bedsprings were audible, then a loud growl.

"They are." Calen agreed. The conversation lapsed, and the noises continued upstairs.

"So, you work at the base?" Her question seemed motivated by a desire to break the silence rather than to engage with him. Calen didn't mind as long as she was actually talking to him.

"Yeah. I'm a paramedic, but mostly I work on the trucks."

"So you're good with your hands?" Cheyenne asked, then realizing the double entendre, made a frustrated face, probably thinking that he was going to make a lewd joke.

Deciding against causing offense, Calen opted for a pleasant conversation instead.

"Yup, I can fix pretty much anything with an engine," he said. "What about you?"

"I work at the Tasty Arrangements," she volunteered.

Calen nodded, familiar with the store that put fruit into arrangements. Calen knew of several guys who sent them to their full moon companions every month, but he never had. Not that he didn't enjoy women and respect them, but he had no interest in wasting energy doing something like that for someone whom he wasn't interested in keeping around long-term.

It was just his luck that the girl he decided to keep worked there, so he would have to find another way to show his interest. Traditionally, he would bring her food and leave it on her doorstep, or take her out to eat, but he had a feeling that she wasn't to the point of appreciating that quite yet, so he would save it for when she was ready... or at least until his eyes didn't still sting from the drink she'd thrown in his face.

"Do you enjoy working there?"

"I love it. I especially love working around the full moon. It's so satisfying to know that what I'm making will make people happy, and maybe help them find love."

Watching her load the last dishes into the dishwasher and start it, he noticed the remaining unwashed big dishes.

"That's a tall order for fruit and chocolate," he commented.

She bristled, and he immediately regretted his choice of phrase. He'd just been trying to make conversation, not be insulting about her job. The chief had given him a second opportunity to bond with her, and he was fucking it up - again.

"Some people like that kind of thing," she said stiffly.

"I didn't mean anything by it. I meant that it's a lot of pressure to put on you, that's all. Here, I'll wash, you dry?" he offered.

"I can wash," she said, recoiling as he took a step near her, glaring at him.

"I don't want you to ruin your nails, they're pretty," he complimented, trying to make up for the idiotic comment about her job.

They hadn't been done on their full moon coupling, and he wondered if she'd gotten them done for her date. He decided he didn't want to know.

"Oh. Okay, yeah, thanks."

"Yup."

They'd finished everything in quick order, setting the scorched chicken pan to soak. They were wrapping up just as there was a dramatic scream and the unmistakable sound of two sets of feet running down the steps. Having no desire to see their alpha in any kind of undignified state with his mate, they hastily made their exit.

Cheyenne bit back a smile as she locked the kitchen door and Calen thought maybe they were making progress after all.

CHAPTER THIRTEEN

CHEYENNE

*C*heyenne shivered in her jacket, reaching down with clumsy fingers to zip it up.

"Where do you live?" Calen asked when they were off the front porch, heading down the sidewalk.

"No offense, but I'm not sure that I want to tell you," she said.

She arched an eyebrow and gave him a look, letting him know exactly how she felt about him knowing where she lived. Pinehurst was a very small town, so it wouldn't take him long to find out if he really wanted to find out, but she wasn't going to tell him and make this easy for him. She'd been on a lovely date and he'd ruined it so he could put some bullshit claim on her? No, she wasn't going to make it easy for him at all.

She'd given him a chance, and he hadn't impressed her. She would rather spend her time and energy on a guy she did like, someone like Matt.

"How could that *not* be offensive?" He asked, turning his head to her, his face tight with irritation.

"Well, you did just crash my date and ran him off by enacting some bullshit old-school courting rule that no one fucking follows, so I guess I don't care if it's offensive," she said, shrugging.

"He chose to run off. He could have stayed and fought for you. If it had been me, I would have fought for you until I couldn't stand."

She didn't try to hide her eye roll at just how over the top he was. Sheesh. Sophie had tried to tell her that Alphas were usually alpha-holes and encouraged her to go for a nice beta, like Matt, but had Cheyenne listened? Of course not. She thought Sophie was just being weird because she was an omega and she was scared of alphas over-powering her.

"I'm sure you would, just to prove a point," she said, putting her hands in her pockets when he looked at her like he might reach for her.

"I want you," he said.

"Yeah, and why is that, exactly? The other night wasn't that memorable, and you didn't even know my name until like an hour ago."

"You ever get cravings?" Calen asked.

"Yeah."

"It's like that, but more."

"What do you mean?" she asked, eying him warily.

A few of the guys in town had imprinted. Maybe Calen had too. Cheyenne cringed at the thought, then dismissed it. She wasn't like Blake's sister, Emma, who was a human. When Blake's work partner had imprinted on her, she hadn't understood the bond or known what it was until the chief had told her.

Cheyenne would know if they had a fated mate's bond. Carefully, she felt around her mind.

It's not there, her wolf said, amused.

I was just checking.

Nothing to find. He's just a male with a big dick and an ego to match, Hazel said.

Cheyenne heard that certain wolves were talkative, constantly conversing in their human's minds. Cheyenne rarely heard Hazel speak, and when she did, she didn't mince words.

Do you like him? Cheyenne ventured.

I do, her wolf said. *But you don't. If you want the beta, it's your choice. I like Ryne. I don't know the Beta's wolf well enough to make a judgement. Besides, I don't have to deal with him if I don't want to.*

When she looked up, Calen was waiting for her attention.

"Sorry," she said, out of habit.

"No need to apologize, I have a wolf too. I know how they can be," he said, offering her an understanding smile.

"I used to do a contest with my brother when we were kids in the lake. We'd see who could hold our breath underwater the longest. Being near you is like that first breath you take when you come up for air. It isn't joy or happiness, but the high when you can fill your lungs with air- you're that," Calen said.

"Oh." Her first thought was to share that line with Shelby, envisioning Shelby's swooning reaction. Her second thought was that he probably used that line all the time on girls, which sent the warm fuzzy feeling she had right down the drain.

"So. Can I walk you home?"

"No."

"You'll disobey the alpha?" He asked, eyes widening.

Her wolf reasoned that their alpha hadn't exactly ordered it, Miss Linda had.

"Yeah. You can tattle to him if you like," Cheyenne smirked. "In fact, I'll wait here if you want to interrupt him and Miss Linda."

"Cheyenne…" she thought he was still standing there. She looked back over her shoulder to see him several paces behind, hands in his jacket pockets.

"Stop following me," she snapped. He didn't respond, just trailing behind her with a huff, and Cheyenne rolled her eyes skyward. "Fine."

She pulled out her phone and called Matt.

"Hey. You wanna meet at my place? Okay, I'll call you. Just let me lose my stalker and I'll be there."

"Cheyenne, if you invite him over, you're going to force us to fight again," Calen said, sighing.

"You are making a choice. I'm making mine," she replied.

"I wish I had a choice. For three weeks I've been trying to convince myself that I should forget you because believe me, I know how crazy it is to be out of your mind over a girl whose name you don't even know. Especially one who seems to despise you."

Cheyenne gave Calen the most disdainful look she could manage.

"Wow. Your ego is so big it's clearly not letting you see this situation clearly, so let me spell this out for you. I've spent very little time thinking about you in the past few weeks. The fact that you think that I despise you just shows how big of an ego you have, because that requires a level of energy I just don't have for you. You would be better off chasing after some girl who wants you to be interested."

She pulled out her phone and sent a quick text to Matt.

CHEYENNE

Hey, I'm at the corner by the chief's house.

She heard Matt's truck coming down the street and smirked. Calen reached into his jacket pocket, frowned, and patted down his jeans pockets as well. Cheyenne stepped to the edge of the sidewalk and watched Calen with amusement, holding up a hand in greeting to Matt as his truck pulled up in front of her, Matt eying Calen warily.

Calen looked up and glowered at Matt's truck, then gave Cheyenne a narrow look.

"By the way, you left your keys at the Beckett's and I locked the door on the way out, so you may have to interrupt their making up so they can let you back in if you want them back. See you around!" Wiggling her fingers, she climbed up into Matt's pickup.

Calen cursed as Cheyenne laughed and got into her car, gratified by the frustration on Calen's face as she pulled away.

Matt's hand glided across the console to grasp her hand, raising an eyebrow in inquiry.

"So, how'd that go?" He asked, tilting his head back over his shoulder to where they'd left Calen standing on the sidewalk.

"Apparently the chief isn't going to put a stop to this, so he has a year to court me," Cheyenne said, rolling her eyes.

"Seriously?"

"Seriously," Cheyenne said. "Miss Linda said that it's basically what he did when he courted her, so he thinks it would be hypocritical to say Calen can't do it."

Matt sighed heavily and Cheyenne's chest tightened. She slid her hand out of his and bit her lip.

"Look, I know this is a lot of drama, and this isn't what you signed up for," Cheyenne said, resigning herself to the idea that she could just use Patrick and Brian as sperm donors to eliminate the problem of Calen interrupting any future dates, or attempts to make a baby.

"It's not, but it's not your fault that Merrick is a prick," Matt said, reaching for her hand and pulling her arm, so it rested back on the console in his. "So, unless you've changed your mind, I'd still like to give this a chance."

"I haven't changed my mind," she said.

"Alright, then."

They drove home in companionable silence and Matt walked her to the door, his body close behind hers as she fumbled with her keys. When her front door was unlocked, Cheyenne felt Matt at her back, his breath warm in her ear.

"I was looking forward to sharing a meal with you." His voice, low and soft, made her body flutter low in her core. "We'll have to reschedule that part, and I understand if you just want to start fresh another night."

"It's not like we haven't fucked before," she said with a little breathy laugh, hoping he wasn't going to try to be a gentleman about their courtship. Rather embarrassingly, the fight over her, while annoying her, had also aroused her and left her needier than she cared to admit.

She wanted the dating experience but she needed sex, too. If he had some noble ideas about having to 'do this properly,' she was going to have to use her body to readjust his expectations. Cheyenne pressed back against him, her tight jeans grinding against his erection.

"It's true, but I want you to know that I really do want to be good to you. I'm not just here for the sex," Matt assured, his hands resting on her hips, pushing her away slightly.

"Matt, I appreciate that, but right now, in this moment, I *really* need some sex," she said, letting her wolf's energy out just a little.

Matt grinned and said in her ear.

"Then let me inside and I'll fuck you until the only thing you remember about tonight was how good my dick felt inside of you."

Cheyenne shivered, but she wasn't cold. She fumbled with her keys as Matt stepped back up against her back, pulling her hips tight against his hard body. He growled a little in her ear and she practically whimpered

"Are you going to be a good girl for me? Show me how good you cum on my dick?"

"Yes," she breathed.

"Good," he said, taking her earlobe in his mouth, sucking hard on it.

"God, stop, just… hang on," she said.

"Do you really want me to stop?" He teased, moving his right hand under her shirt, and his left moving between her legs, using the seam of her jeans to stimulate her clit, working to find the right spot until she gasped.

"There, that's what I want," he said, chuckling as she dropped her keys.

She had to bend over to retrieve them, but she had the feeling that as soon as she did, he was going to make her regret it.

Sure enough, as soon as her head was down, the pressure on her clit increased, the palm of his hand grinding against her entrance, serving as a reminder of just how empty she was. She moaned and he rubbed more, making her pant.

"Matt," she whined.

"Aren't you going to let me in, baby momma?" Matt asked lightly.

"You're gonna have to give me a minute," she said, straightening, and trying to move away.

"I'm going to give you all night if you're good," he said,

"Matt," she breathed as she felt the beginnings of an orgasm building in her core, making her spine tingle.

"Everything okay over there?" A friendly voice called.

Cheyenne looked up, her cheeks blazing as she realized she'd just orgasmed outside on her front porch with her neighbor listening. Her neighbor who was one of Pinehurst's deputies no less.

Not that Scott hadn't heard her come before, they'd spent plenty of nights having quickies to scratch the itch before Cheyenne got serious about settling down and making a family. When they weren't enjoying one another as casual sex partners, they were close neighbors, sharing gossip and hanging out over a bowl of popcorn and mugs of steaming tea.

"Yeah- everything's fine! Just having trouble with the door," she called.

"You need a hand?"

"I've got it now, thanks Scott!"

"Yup!" Scott called back, his voice tinged with laughter.

Cheyenne unlocked and opened the front door, then tumbled inside the house while Matt followed on her heels.

CHAPTER FOURTEEN

CHEYENNE

*T*hey barely made it into the house before Matt's tongue was in her ear, his hands undoing her jeans as they tumbled in through the open door.

"I've been wondering what kind of panties you've been wearing all night," he said as she moaned, drawing him into the house. He reached down the front of her pants and froze when he realized there was no fabric underneath her jeans. His hands only touched her trimmed hair.

Cheyenne grinned as she saw his wolf take over, his eyes going slightly feral as Matt spun her around so her back was to the wall and grabbed her jeans, yanking them down, jerking her flats off before snatching her pant leg off her leg like it personally offended him. Before she could react, he'd pushed her against the wall, grabbed her calf, and placed her leg on his shoulder, giving him access to her pussy.

"All night you weren't wearing any fucking panties?" He growled, then his hands spread her wide and his mouth found her clit.

She couldn't find words to reply as he licked and sucked her, pleasuring her with his fingers until she was a quivering mess.

"Matt," she begged. "I'm going to fall."

"Don't," he ordered. "You may not move from this spot until you come on my face at least once."

He played with her until she was so desperate for her release that her hands found his hair and gripped it at the roots as incoherent words and noises fell from her lips, trying to beg him not to stop, to give her more.

When he finally slid two fingers inside of her soaking pussy and crooked them just so, she fell apart, throwing her head back with a cry as her leg that was thrown over his shoulder gripped him. As she came back down from her orgasm, she realized her leg was clamped around his head, holding him against her.

"Oh, moon, I'm so sorry," she laughed, somewhat unsteadily moving her leg from his shoulder.

"Why?" Matt asked as he flashed her a supremely satisfied grin. Catching sight of his disheveled hair, she laughed again.

"Let me," she said, reaching to smooth it out.

He caught her wrists and stood, shaking his head.

"Why? I'm hoping you grab it again when I'm putting a baby in you," he said, walking backwards down the hall.

"Matt?"

"Yeah?"

"My bedroom's the other way," she said with a slight giggle.

He chuckled.

"I was trying to be so smooth," he admitted with a rueful grin.

"You're very smooth," she assured.

CHEYENNE WASN'T sure her legs would work ever again. Matt had, as he said it, made his best attempt to get her pregnant. He'd suggested naughtily in her ear as he'd taken her roughly from behind that the more times she orgasmed, the more likely she was to get pregnant, and while she wasn't certain of the science behind it, she was absolutely not going to argue with him.

"Would you like me to stay?" Matt asked when he'd recovered his breath enough to speak.

They were both sweaty, sprawled out, not touching one another on her bed. Her pillows and blankets were scattered around the room. As their enthusiastic coupling had heated them, she'd been too hot to tolerate the bunched-up fabric beneath her.

"I thought you had work in the morning?" She asked, turning her head, and making a face as she moved her hair that had plastered with sweat to the back of her neck.

"I do, but I don't want to just have sex with you and leave."

"Matt, we're grown-ups with grown-up jobs. I get it. I don't need you to stay and hold my hand instead of sleeping where you'll get the best rest."

"Okay, I'm going to head out then, as long as you're sure?"

"Definitely," she said, offering him a reassuring smile.

"Okay then." He leaned forward and placed one hand on her stomach, sliding it up until he clasped her cheek, planting a soft kiss on her lips. "Thank you for a lovely evening, all the drama notwithstanding."

"Thank you," she said.

"I'll see you soon," he promised.

He went to the bathroom to clean up. When he emerged, she was stripping the sheets off the bed.

"I can help," he suggested.

"Matt, go home and get some sleep," she said.

He chuckled.

"You're going to make a great mother," he murmured in her ear, kissing the hair just behind it before moving away to get dressed.

Cheyenne's cheeks heated at the praise, and then she threw on her favorite powder blue cotton bathrobe and followed Matt out into the main body of the house so she could grab her spare sheets from the linen closet and put the old ones in the wash.

MATT SAID goodbye and left her, telling her he would text her when he got home, and admonishing her to get some rest. Even though she probably should have been tired, she knew sleep was far away. She'd always been a night owl, and even though six am would come early, Cheyenne wouldn't even bother trying to lay down for a few more hours.

When she went to plug her phone in, she had a few texts waiting.

SCOTT

So...spill.

Is he our lucky baby daddy?

I thought he was gonna fuck you right there on the porch. *fire emoji*

Cheyenne laughed and checked her other messages. Scott could wait for a second.

MATT

Thank you for a lovely night.

I really am sorry about leaving. I needed clothes.

CHEYENNE

It's really okay, and thank YOU. I had a lovely time, minus the interruption.

When she'd texted Matt back, she switched back to her thread with Scott.

CHEYENNE

If you want all the deets, I'll make the tea, you make the snacks?

SCOTT

Deal.

Five minutes later, her front door opened.

"Alright, get out here and spill! I heard Calen and Matt had a fight outside behind Lillingtons, is that true?"

"Just you wait," Cheyenne laughed as she came out of the

bedroom.

"So wait," Scott said, shaking his head. "You mean to tell me, Calen *claimed* you? Like, old school, 'Hey, this bitch is mine for the next year' kind of claimed you?"

"Yup," Cheyenne said, taking a long draw on her hot tea.

"And the chief just... let him?"

"Yup," Cheyenne agreed slowly, ruminating in her frustration.

"Gross," Scott said.

"Right?" Cheyenne sat up.

"That surprises the hell out of me," Scott confessed. "Usually, the chief is really fair. I wonder if it's because he wants to retire."

"What does that have anything to do with me?"

"There's a rumor he doesn't want to step down and hand the pack over to someone who doesn't have a mate. Maybe he thinks if you and Calen get together, he can hand the pack over to him."

Cheyenne shook her head and Scott continued, taking a handful of the popcorn for himself.

"Look, I don't know if that's what's going on, but I know he and Calen are tight. The chief has the usual meetings with the bio alphas, but Calen working up at the base gives him a lot of access. Now he's letting Calen claim you even though it's not the Middle Ages, and no one does that any more? Sounds to me like he might be trying to be in Calen's corner."

"That's bullshit," Cheyenne said, then added. "If it's true."

"So what are you going to do?" Scott asked.

"Well, I can tell you what I'm not going to do," Cheyenne declared, sitting back on the couch and propping her feet up on the coffee table. "I'm not going to give Calen Merrick a chance to make me his mate."

Hazel growled her agreement and Cheyenne stayed up late talking to Scott. He finally left well into the night when the waning moon was high in the sky.

CHAPTER FIFTEEN

CALEN

*T*here was no way in hell Calen was going to interrupt the chief and his mate making up, so Calen shoved his hands deeper inside of his coat pockets and trudged back to the base. His apartment was locked, and it was easier to shower at the base and crash in one of the apartments they kept upstairs for crew and family than go back to the Chief's house for his truck, keys, and jacket in the morning.

As he trudged, Calen stewed about the evening. While he'd been enjoying the nice end of the evening, she'd been letting him leave his keys locked in the house and texting Matt. He wanted to be irritated, but Ryne pointed out that it was hardly reasonable for Calen to be any kind of way about her reaction when he'd interrupted another man whom she wanted to court her in the first place.

Whose side are you on? Calen asked.

The side that doesn't end up with us looking like fools, Ryne retorted. *And the side that means we get a full night's sleep instead of trudging around town like a homeless vagrant because you're too distracted by a female to notice you don't have your keys,*

"Hey, thought you left," Lawson said as Calen walked through the front door.

"I did," Calen said. "Are any of the rooms upstairs occupied? I need a place to crash."

"Nope, they're all open," his captain informed him with an assessing look.

"Can I have five?" Calen asked without elaborating about why he smelled like a fruity alcohol, was covered in said sticky beverage, and why he now needed a room for the night.

"Sure thing. I'll grab you the key."

Luckily, the medic who was his counterpart on this shift wasn't in the room they shared, so Calen was able to walk in and grab a set of spare clothes before heading upstairs to room five to shower. Some of the apartments didn't have a shower, and while normally he didn't mind the communal bathroom, he needed some privacy.

Hot water cascaded over him, washing away the sticky mess, warming his muscles he'd held tight with the tension he'd had since watching Cheyenne climb into Matt Griffith's truck.

Once he was washed off, Calen grabbed his dick and pictured Cheyenne. He'd intended to replay the time they'd spent together on the last full moon, but instead, he found himself thinking about her standing at the kitchen sink at the Alphas's house, her hair a little mussed, looking put together enough for a date, but in that moment, content to be domestic.

The pleased look she'd given him when he'd offered to wash the dishes because he didn't want her to ruin her nails was seared into his mind, even more than how he'd enjoyed her in his bed. It hadn't been a polite smile, it was genuine, and he had an ache in his chest thinking about how much wanted to make her smile like that again.

He held his shaft in his right hand, leaning on his opposite forearm, shuddering as he pictured her. Hell, he wanted a lot more than just her smiling at him. He wanted her at *his* kitchen sink, her belly big with his child as he washed and she dried dishes as they chatted about their day while they cleaned up from the dinner he would make for her. Afterwards, they would go sit on their front porch. This time, instead of sitting far away from him, she would curl up in his lap with her head resting on his shoulder as they watched the stars come out.

They would go inside, him carrying her into the bedroom and laying her down in his bed, their bed, and she would look like an angel, her hair fanned out on the pillow, her brown eyes shining up at him with a look of seductive mischief.

At the image, his balls tightened and pleasure shot through his whole body. Calen let out a primal groan as he spilled his seed against the shower wall. When he'd emptied himself, he sighed. His hand was a poor substitute for her.

As he climbed into the bed, Ryne spoke into his mind.

So, are we going to acknowledge that was the weirdest thing you've ever jerked off to? Ryne asked.

No, Calen thought back.

Ryne was silent for a while and Calen was nearly asleep when Ryne's mental voice was soft.

You really do want her, don't you? Ryne asked. *Not just for sex.*

Obviously, Calen thought back, his mind half-claimed by sleep. *What's your point?*

I don't get it, but if she's the one you choose to be our mate, alright, Ryne thought back, sending his warm support through their bond.

Calen had to fight back the darkness of sleep to form a coherent reply.

I don't get it either, he thought back. After a moment of silence, he sighed. *Thank you.*

Go to sleep, human. We'll figure out how to make our mate fall in love with us tomorrow, Ryne thought back.

Calen was already asleep.

CALEN WAS ALMOST BACK to the base after transporting one of their older frequent flyers to the emergency room at Mountain Regional in Red River when a call came out.

"Medic 7, be en route emergency traffic in reference to a twenty-four-

year-old female with traumatic injuries. The patient is conscious and breathing at this time; bleeding is uncontrolled."

Calen didn't look up from the report he was working on.

"Medic 7 en route. Any further information on this call?" Arion's voice came over the radio.

"Subject is in a barn. The same has been impaled. FD and PD en route. No further at this time."

Calen blinked and looked at Burgess, who frowned.

"Impaled? Like impaled?" Calen's EMT Mike Burgess asked, eyes widening comically as his face lit up at the prospect of a real call.

After a shift where he and his partner had spent five hours sitting in the truck on the county line on standby in case the adjoining county had too many calls when they were short-staffed and busy, and then one call for back pain, Calen wasn't going to turn down an opportunity for something interesting.

"Wanna go see?" Calen asked, curious himself.

"Heck, yeah!"

"Alright, let's go see if they need a hand."

When they got to the barn, paramedic Arion Easton and his EMT Aiden were triaging the patient in the back of their rig. A firefighter was ready to take them to the ambulance

"Hey, man, just checking in to see if you needed a hand," Calen said, opening the side door of Arion's ambulance.

"Nah, we're good," Arion said.

"Hey, Calen." A familiar brown chaotic jumble of coiled hair flounced as the patient raised her head, revealing her face as she offered him a pained but bright smile. One of his deputy friends' little sisters, a little firecracker of an activist whose favorite hobby was finding new causes she could advocate for.

"Hey, Brooke," he greeted. "What'd you do?"

"I scraped myself on a nail," she said, grimacing as Arion worked on the spot.

"That's no good," he glanced back, noticing the placement of the wound. "What'd you do, sit on it?"

"Yup, ripped right through my favorite leggings," she said with a watery smile, whimpering as she reached for Arion's EMT's hand.

Calen glanced over and Aiden offered Arion an apologetic smile but didn't let go of Brooke's hand. While technically a member of the Pinehurst pack, Aiden and Brooke were in a group of shifters that almost acted like their own micro-pack under another one of the town's bio alphas, Everett Hopper.

Arion shook his head that he didn't care. He might not like that he didn't have an extra set of hands, but Arion understood the need to support your pack.

"I got you," Aiden said, looking from her face to Arion's with concern.

Calen caught Arion's eye, who nodded to indicate she would be fine and there was no reason to worry.

"Well, looks like you'll live," Aiden joked with Brooke as he held her hand.

"You're a jerk. Of course, I'm going to live," she said, but she offered him a watery smile.

"Is everything good here? You don't need a hand?"

"I could use another set of hands," Arion said, with a meaningful glance at Brooke and Aiden's clasped ones.

The back of the ambulance opened and Brooke squealed in surprise, jumping.

"Hey," Arion snapped at the intruder.

"Brooklyn?" Trey McQuilken, one of the owners of the quarry on the outskirts of town, stepped up into the ambulance, his gaze sweeping over his young mate with concern.

"Sir, I'm going to need you to step outside until we're finished here," Arion instructed, adjusting the drape over Brooke's backside.

"That's my mate. I'm not going anywhere," Trey replied, his jaw set as his massive frame filled the back of the ambulance's back doorway.

Calen quickly took stock of the situation, grabbed Aiden's tablet, and gestured to his left to the side door he stood next to.

"Actually," Calen cut in smoothly before the bear shifter could get worked up. "If you're her mate, you can help us with the paperwork we need to fill out. Can you step out here so we can take care of that? I don't want to distract her medic while he's working on her."

Trey nodded.

"I'll be back if you're alright," Trey said to the back of Brooke's head. The big man's eyes looked at Arion's EMT holding his friend's hand and narrowed.

"Burgess, give Arion a hand in the back," Calen said to his EMT after climbing back down.

"Got it."

Calen took as long as possible to do the paperwork for Brooke. Trey McQuilken was anxious to get back to his and his brothers' shared mate. The usually cool and reserved man stripped off his coat and asked more than once if Calen was sure his mate was alright in there. Calen assured him that Arion would call out if there were any problems. Calen had no reason to think there would be issues. Arion didn't seem worried about the spot, and most likely they would take her for a tetanus shot and an antibiotic rinse, and possibly some stitches at the local ER.

"They ready to head out?" Calen asked.

Trey went to walk to the back door of the ambulance, but Calen stopped him.

"Mr. McQuilken," he said. "I'm sorry. We can't let you ride in the back. It's protocol, but you're welcome to follow the rig to the hospital."

When Trey looked mutinous, Calen looked at Trey's brother Rory, who had arrived mid-questionnaire and lowered his voice, hoping to talk some sense into him. Newly mated shifters were notoriously edgy, and Calen was sure that having another male with his hands all over their mate's ass didn't help matters. Calen knew, like the rest of the first responders in the county did, that while Rory was one of the nicest men you'd ever meet, his bear was near-feral, an extremely aggressive giant brown bear. Calen wanted nothing to do with Rory's bear making an unwanted appearance.

"She isn't emergent. The only reason she needs to go to the hospital is for a tetanus shot and a couple of stitches. She'll be alright,"

Calen assured in a professional tone meant to instill confidence. "If it were my mate, I would trust Arion with her."

Our 'mate' would probably hit us if we showed up and tried to climb in the rig with her, Ryne thought dryly.

Isn't that the truth? Calen thought with a chuckle, wondering what Cheyenne was up to.

Rory nodded and thanked him, while Trey stalked off without another word, heading purposefully to his car as Arion jumped into the front seat to take her to Regional. The McQuilken brothers walked off to their car, Trey jumping into the driver's seat, trailing the ambulance closely out of the field.

"Hey man," Scott said with a friendly tip of his chin as he walked by, holding his tablet for making his report of the incident.

"Hey, did you see your sister?"

"Oh yeah, I got here before Medic 7 did. I figured between her mates and Aiden, she had enough emotional support."

"Yeah, she's in good hands," Calen agreed.

"So, you and Cheyenne, huh?" Scott asked with a grin.

"Well, sort of," Calen admitted with a little laugh. "I'd say yes, but I think she's more on the fence."

"Seemed that way last time we talked," Scott agreed.

"You know her?" Calen asked, trying to keep a note of jealousy out of his voice.

"Well, yeah, she's my next-door neighbor," Scott informed Calen, then took a half-step back, raising his hands slightly. "Don't go hitting me or anything. I haven't touched her since she decided she wanted to get pregnant."

"She *what?*"

CHAPTER SIXTEEN

CHEYENNE

"*I* just feel weird being on camera. Why can't we use Shelby or Ben? Ben's the owner," Cheyenne pointed out.

"Because our target market is mostly males, and Shelby dresses like she's a homeless dike who rolled out of bed to come to work," Sophie said.

"It's true, I'm not here to attract men, and you're much prettier than Ben," Shelby agreed.

Cheyenne rolled her eyes.

"So, you just go around and do your thing, and I'll take pictures. Sometimes I'll ask you to stop or pause and look at me. It's really no big deal."

Even though she was uncomfortable with the idea, having Sophie there to take her picture for their new social media accounts Sophie was managing was actually a blast. Sophie was all compliments and smiles as Cheyenne worked, making her feel like she was the star of a photo shoot, not just someone who was working on making fruit arrangements for a customer and prepping fruit for the next day's orders.

"Okay, I think I have everything I need," Sophie said, scrolling through pictures of Cheyenne on her camera.

"Ooh, let me see," Cheyenne said.

"Nope, you can see the finished product!" Sophie informed her, turning away and clicking the display screen off.

"Hey! What if I'm ugly and I have my eyes half-closed like some kind of deranged troll mid-orgasm?"

"Firstly, nothing about you is troll-like. Second, I'm not going to post a picture where you look anything but stunning," Sophie informed her. Giving Cheyenne a slow once-over, she grinned. "Not that it should be hard, but I promise I'll make you look good, okay?"

"Alright," Cheyenne said, pursing her lips as she rinsed off the cutting board she'd just used for slicing the flower-shaped pineapple pieces.

"Trust me, alright?"

"I trust you."

"Alright then. On another note, we should hang out. I've been missing you lately."

"Yeah, we should! Hey! How about we go to the bake sale next weekend? I have the day off. We can hang and do a girls' night instead of messing around with stupid boys on the full moon."

"Matt's working, isn't he?" Sophie guessed with a laugh.

"Totally is. He usually volunteers to work the full moon so the guys with mates can go spend it with them. He'd already signed up for the shift before we started talking. I told him I didn't mind."

Sophie gave her a funny look but agreed that it would be fun to have a girl's night.

"I'll text you," Cheyenne promised.

Later that night, Cheyenne was feeling frisky. She'd forgotten how nice it was to have a boyfriend you could just text when you needed sex.

Since he'd interrupted her date, Calen had made himself blessedly scarce. The chances of her getting pregnant when the moon wasn't full were pretty slim, but it couldn't hurt to practice, right? Her body certainly seemed to think so.

She thought of the authority Calen's wolf had held over her, and her core clenched. Shit, he was right. There was something there between them, but she'd be damned before she let some man dictate her life to her. She wanted a man who could dominate her in the bedroom, not one who was a domineering ass. Right? Her treacherous vagina was wet at the thought of Calen bursting down the door, dragging her to the bedroom... her hand was sliding down inside of her pajamas before she caught herself.

Sex with Calen hadn't been all that great. He talked a big game, but it had been Matt who had her screaming his name last full moon. She grabbed her phone and texted him before she could chicken out. Technically, if Calen was courting her, then if he found another guy here, he could challenge him to a fight - another fight. Matt was a great guy, but she didn't like the idea of putting two guys against each other for her amusement. Then again... if Calen was going to be here, he would be here already, wouldn't he?

CHEYENNE

Hey- want to come over?

MATT

I shouldn't.

Cheyenne sent a picture of herself in a lace teddy, the tight bodice pressing her breasts up

MATT

...you're going to get me in trouble.

CHEYENNE

Oh. I thought you were being flirty before. I'm sorry.

MATT

I was. Fuck it. I'm on my way. Unlock the back door.

Cheyenne shimmied out of her pajama bottoms and was working on lighting a fire in the fireplace when she heard a car door, and then a heavy hand knocking on her front door.

"Hey, I thought you said- what are you doing here?" It was Calen, not Matt, who was standing in the doorway.

"I was going to see if you wanted to go out," he took in her appearance, pupils dilating as they traveled over her skimpy outfit.

The cold air from the early spring night drew her nipples into tight points and sent goosebumps over her exposed skin. Calen swallowed hard, adjusting his jeans before speaking in a low, ragged voice.

"Or… we could stay in."

"I'm not doing anything with you," she said, putting her hand on her hip. "I don't like you."

She needed to get rid of him right now. Calen sniffed and tore his eyes away from her body to look over her shoulder and spoke matter-of-factly.

"Your fire is going out."

"Oh, fuck!"

Calen pushed past her and knelt in front of her fireplace.

"Calen, you need to go."

"Shut the door. You're letting the warm air out." He took up the lighter and lit a small piece of paper on fire, laying it near a small bundle of kindling, breathing life back into her fire.

"I'm serious, I'm going to -"

"If you're going to say you're going to have them send a county car to escort me off the premises, good luck. By pack law, I'm allowed to be here as long as we're courting. In the meantime, are you watching this?" He indicated the TV as he slipped out of his boots.

"Get. Out." She didn't know if it was true about it being pack law, but she didn't care. Matt was going to show up any minute in wolf form.

"You don't listen very well," he commented, easing back onto the couch like he belonged there. "This couch is nice. Looks like something my grandmother would buy, but damn if it isn't one of the comfiest things I've ever sat on. I have a right to be where you are, firecracker."

"You have no right to be in my living room!"

A scratching sounded at the back door and Calen's eyes darkened.

"You are mine. I claimed you. If there's someone else making a move on what's mine, you can be damn sure I'll defend it. Answer the door, Cheyenne."

"Fine." She walked to the back door.

She heard him rise from the couch behind her. She intended to open the back door just enough to step outside and tell Matt to just go home, but as soon as the door opened, Matt slunk past in wolf form.

Calen bent down and scooped her boyfriend by the scruff, hauling him up off the floor like a misbehaving puppy.

"Open the door, firecracker," he said calmly, while Matt's wolf snarled in Calen's grasp.

With resignation, she opened the door back. Calen took a step outside and dumped Matt's wolf over the railing of her back porch.

Before she could think twice about it, she closed and bolted the door, locking Calen outside.

"Cheyenne - let me in," Calen insisted.

"Fuck you!"

"I'd love to, baby, but you locked me out. Open up and I'll be happy to oblige," he joked.

Her body clenched at the idea. She swore she heard him chuckle like he knew what she was thinking.

"Leave me alone!"

"You going to tell me you'd rather be alone than have me worship you all night long?" he asked in a challenge that made her both weak at the knees and defiant.

Damn him. Spending the full moon alone was something she'd never done. As an alpha female, her instinct to breed was strong. She could have her pick of the male shifters. The drive to mate was already calling her, making her skin tingle.

"Cheyenne, firecracker, please," he called through the door.

She was so tempted. Her body was on fire. She felt so empty and desperate with need. She'd just moved toward the door, her fingers brushing against the door handle when Calen spoke again.

"You know you're going to give in. Don't make it harder than it has to be."

Oh, hell no. That streak of defiance she and her wolf shared flared to life, burning hotter than the fire currently heating her living room.

"The only thing I'm giving in to tonight is my dildo," she informed him.

"Can I at least have my boots?"

"Are you going to leave?"

"No."

"Then no."

When he didn't respond, she went to her bedroom and opened the second drawer of her dresser, rifling around through the toys for her favorites, then yanked the entire drawer of the dresser and carried it out to the living room.

"Cheyenne, what the hell are you doing?" He asked, looking through the window to the side of her front door with a frown.

"I told you, my dildo." She set the entire drawer down on the coffee table and walked to the window, flipping him off before closing the blinds. "But you're more than welcome to stand out in the cold and listen."

CHAPTER SEVENTEEN

CALEN

*C*alen set down the free weights, blowing out a hard breath. He stretched and glanced down at his phone, then shook his head. Fuck, he wanted Cheyenne to call, text, anything, even if she was mad at him... which she probably was.

He hadn't spoken with her directly since Scott had casually dropped the bomb that Cheyenne was trying to get pregnant, and ever since then, he'd been lifting like he was training for a competition, and stalking her like a psychotic whack job.

He was beginning to think this whole thing was a bad idea. Maybe he was crazy, but he'd really thought that his being persistent and not giving in to her resistance was what she wanted, what she needed. Maybe he'd been mistaken, and he was just wasting his time and effort, not to mention keeping her from being with the man she'd actually chosen to be with.

He grimaced at the thought, then picked up his phone, unable to stop himself.

CALEN

> Hey beautiful, you coming to the bake sale today?

He put his phone down and picked up the free weights, doing another set of chest presses. His phone buzzed in his pocket and he pushed through the rest of the set with a grin spread across his face.

FUTURE WIFE

Yes, I'm coming with a date.

CALEN

Oh?

Calen's grin faded, and he leveled a dark look at his phone screen, his chest tightening in the all-too-familiar spiral of jealousy that had become his new normal when it came to anyone else spending time with his woman. Then he remembered Matt was out of town to see his sick mother and the coil in his chest eased. Maybe she was coming with one of the Lawson guys and calling it a date. That would be fine, as long as Brian wasn't a prospective baby daddy for her.

He'd heard that Patrick and Brian were looking for a shifter woman to have a child with, and he knew Cheyenne enjoyed a friend- ship with them from the gossip he'd heard. He'd felt safe, knowing that on the nights she went to dinner at their house, Brian was in a committed relationship and Patrick was only into men.

Now Calen wondered if this was why she was so standoffish with him. Maybe she was pregnant already.

Could she be pregnant with his baby? She'd said she had protec- tion during their night together, and since shifters couldn't get STDs, he hadn't worn a condom.

The idea of her pregnant with his child sent blood pumping through his body as his heart rate skyrocketed. He pushed out two more sets and finished his workout in a black mood when he realized that if she was pregnant that it could also be Matt's or even Brian's baby. Calen showered, and then went downstairs to the ambulance bay, looking out for Cheyenne's tall frame.

"Hey, who's that?" Owen elbowed Calen, interrupting his thoughts.

Calen looked at the girl Owen indicated. A cute little thing, with brown hair and a yellow dress that screamed innocence. Calen racked his brain, trying to place her for a moment before he remembered where he'd seen her before.

"I think her name's Caitlin. She's a friend of Olivia's," Calen replied.

He'd seen her coming out of Pinehurst's therapist's office several times when he was going in for his own appointments, but that wasn't any of his business. Not that he thought going to a therapist was anything to be ashamed of, but it wasn't his place to talk about it.

"How are things going with your girl?" Owen asked, his eyes still on the girl who was adjusting the velcro on a wrist brace, wincing as she flexed her fingers.

Calen looked at Owen and back at the girl. Owen deserved a good woman; he was usually working too hard to give most women the time of day unless it was the full moon and he and his wolf Finley needed to get a little loving. Owen kept his eyes on the girl, but Calen thought about his own woman with her brown hair.

He was surprised she wasn't here yet, actually. She had answered his text offering her a ride to the bake sale with a selfie of her making a rude hand gesture with her finger. He'd made the photo his background on his phone and thanked her for giving him something cute for his phone wallpaper. He looked back over the texts, just to make sure he hadn't missed her response.

CALEN

Aw, thanks firecracker. I needed a good picture of you for my home screen.

You know, that'll be a great pic to show the grandkids one day.

He'd been hoping to get a rise out of her with the grandkid comment, but either she was driving or he'd taken it too far. He wished he knew which.

"She's stubborn," Calen grinned. "Giving me hell and not showing any signs of letting up."

"Yeah? Has she accepted you courting her yet?" Owen asked, his eyes still fixed on the girl.

"Not at all," Calen said, unperturbed. "She's still acting like I'm satan himself."

Calen reveled in the fact that at least she was responding to his text messages now. She'd been opening them and leaving him on read for over a week, which had been driving him nuts. At least now she was talking, even if it was to argue.

You're unhinged, Ryne observed, without judgment.

You like it that she responds to us too, Calen replied, bristling.

Not like you do, Ryne thought back.

"Man, I don't know how you do it. That would drive me crazy," Owen said.

"Oh, it is. She's still trying to see other guys," Calen said darkly, wondering if she was with Matt right now.

If she wasn't here in fifteen minutes, he was going to go check on her and make sure she wasn't meeting up with Matt again. Checking his watch, he noted that it was 11:52. His woman had until 12:07.

"How's that going for her?" Owen asked with a chuckle.

"Not very well. I ran Matt off the other night." Calen grinned at the memory of him tossing Matt's wolf out of her house. "I've never seen any wolf run so fast."

"Part-time medic, Matt?" Owen clarified.

"Same guy," Calen agreed. "I don't blame him. He's a decent guy, and pheromones are pheromones. He's a Beta; he can't help it. She's got that alpha female blood."

Calen blew out a breath, trying not to think about how he would like to be enjoying that. He wondered how much she'd held herself back the night they were together. He bet when they finally fucked, she would leave him marked to hell, looking like a war victim.

"Yeah. You can only fight biology so much," Owen murmured, his eyes still on the girl.

"Why don't you quit staring and go say hi before she thinks you're a psycho?" Calen asked, elbowing Owen.

"What? Who?" Owen asked, tearing his eyes away for a moment to look at Calen.

"Olivia's friend, who you've been staring at since you came over," Calen pointed out.

"Oh. Well," Owen said, hesitating.

"Man, just go say hi. Seriously," Calen said with a shove and a laugh. "If you don't, someone else will."

Owen walked away and one of the firefighters walked up beside Calen.

"April's a little early for sundress season, but I'm not one to complain," the firefighter said, admiring Caitlin's yellow sundress.

Calen snorted.

"I think that one is spoken for," Calen informed him.

"I was just enjoying the view," the volunteer said with a lustful look at the woman he suspected would be Owen's new woman if Owen had any say in the matter.

Just at that moment, Cheyenne walked around the corner of the bay with one of the omegas, a petite little thing with dyed red hair.

"Indeed," Calen agreed, admiring how Cheyenne looked in her fitted jeans and her t-shirt supporting Aiden and Brooke's band.

Calen walked over to his woman, not making any effort to keep his energy contained. The omega, whose name was Sophie, he recalled, noticed him first, eyes widening and taking a half-step back. He offered her a reassuring smile and Sophie flashed him a nervous one in return, taking another half-step back that put her firmly behind Cheyenne, who looked up from a display of locally made cake pops, sensing her friend's discomfort. Immediately her posture was defensive, her eyes swinging to him, first in defiance, then in annoyance. He grinned when he realized this omega girl must be her date.

"What do you want?" She asked, putting a hand on her hip.

"Good afternoon, Cheyenne," he said pleasantly, and giving the omega a smile and a polite nod, added. "And Sophie."

Cheyenne crossed her arms over her chest, drawing his attention to the way her t-shirt stretched over her curves. She huffed and rolled her eyes.

"Are you ladies looking for something in particular?" Calen asked, directing the question to Sophie since he knew Cheyenne's answer would be unhelpful at best, and he suspected that ignoring her in preference of speaking to her omega friend would get a rise out of her.

"Yes," Sophie admitted with a timid nod.

"What are you looking for?" He asked, his manner turning charming, bordering on flirtatious. Cheyenne huffed, her cheeks coloring.

"We're doing a girl's night. We wanted to come by and get some snacks," Sophie volunteered shyly.

"Why didn't you say so?" Calen said with a grin. "I'll bring a bottle of wine when I drop by."

"You are not invited," Cheyenne said, narrowing her eyes. Despite her tone, Calen saw how her eyes traveled over him, how her pupils dilated with desire.

"No? Is your omega friend going to help take the edge off that empty feeling, firecracker? Can I watch?" He stepped forward, lowering his voice, letting his eyes glaze over Sophie. "I bet she'd rock a strap-on."

Sophie's cheeks turned a color that was charming, and Cheyenne rolled her eyes.

"If you knew me at all, you would know I'm straight," she said, her eyes raking over him with what was supposed to be disgust, but he didn't miss the way her eyes lingered over his pumped muscles.

"Even straight girls experiment," Calen said with a grin. "Besides, if using a dildo solo doesn't make you not straight, using one with a girl-friend doesn't have to either. I don't judge a girl's desperate actions due to lack of dick."

"Who says I haven't gotten any?" Cheyenne challenged.

"You two," Ma's voice cut through the conversation. "I will thank you to remember that you are in public and there are families here."

Cheyenne's cheeks flushed with genuine embarrassment at the rebuke, looking dismayed, then indignant that his comments had gotten her into trouble.

Calen decided the best way to deflect the blame was to keep it up and turn Ma's wrath on himself.

"Well, Ma, I'm trying to make us a family too, but she's not cooperating," Calen joked.

"Be that as it may," Ma said. "There are children present, and I expect you both to act like upstanding representatives of the community, not like horny teenagers who can't keep their foreplay out of the public eye."

Cheyenne's cheeks were flaming hotter than Sophie's, and tears of anger burned in her eyes. Calen's chest tightened and Ryne growled in their mental link.

You should have let me handle it. You're screwing this up about as badly as a man can, Calen.

Oh, thanks Ryne. That's incredibly helpful of you to point out after the fact, Calen snapped.

"I'm sorry," he began, but his woman took a step back.

"Come on," Sophie said, diffusing the tension between the two alphas. "I heard Owen going on about the cookies over this way."

Calen let Cheyenne be pulled away, and he watched her with a sharp eye as they bought their baked goods. He would be staying until the end of his shift, long after the bake sale ended, but he stationed himself near the door so he wouldn't miss when Cheyenne and her companion left.

A little while later, Sophie appeared by the bay door, a watchful eye looking for Cheyenne to return.

"So what exactly does girl's night entail?" Calen asked her. She jumped, and he chuckled.

"Um, I think we were going to watch a movie," she muttered, her cheeks coloring as she glanced away, avoiding his gaze.

"You wouldn't be lying to me, would you, little omega?"

"No," Sophie said, eyes going wide as he hit the nail on the head.

"What else do you and my mate have planned for the evening, Sophie?" He asked, letting the barest hint of his alpha magic trickle into his voice.

Sophie fiddled with the strap of her cross-body bag, not meeting his eye.

"Secrets, hm?" He said in a soft, cajoling tone.

"Leave my omega alone," Cheyenne said with a snarl from beside Sophie.

Cheyenne stepped between them and unhooked her keys from her belt, handing them to Sophie, and instructing her to wait in the car for her. Sophie left without a word.

"Strictly speaking, she's *my* omega," the chief said before Calen could think up something witty to say.

"Yes, chief, I just-" Cheyenne said, gesturing to Calen.

"I'm well aware that Sophie is your companion for the full moon this evening, Cheyenne, but Calen having a conversation with her doesn't give you the right to go around claiming her, unless you're looking to challenge my authority and take my place as the Alpha of this pack. Are you looking to challenge my authority, girl?"

Cheyenne held the Chief's stare for a moment longer than was strictly polite before replying, without lowering her eyes.

"No, sir."

"Then let your language choices reflect that," Jason said, one eyebrow raising.

Cheyenne crossed her arms over her chest, drawing Calen's attention to her breasts. She noticed and rolled her eyes.

"With *all* due respect, alpha, if you hadn't allowed Calen to claim someone who wasn't interested in being claimed, then-" she began.

"Then *you* wouldn't have been disrespectful, is that it?" Jason's voice was sharp. "Cheyenne, did it ever occur to you that I was doing you a favor? You asked me to help you find an alpha that would be a good match for you, and since then you haven't given any of the young bio alphas in our pack the time of day because 'none of them are strong enough leaders for you.'"

Cheyenne opened her mouth, but Jason held up a finger, silencing her protest.

"I made it so that you would be forced to consider if what you say you want, an alpha male, is *really* what you want."

Calen watched silently, a little smugly, until Cheyenne was dismissed and the weight of the alpha's full authority fell on him. He raised his eyes, meeting the Chief's gaze.

"Son," Jason said, blowing his breath out slowly, his wolf looking out of his eyes, boring into Calen's. "We need to talk."

"I won't apologize for courting my mate in public. Ma was out of line, sir."

"I don't know anything about that, but if Ma had something to say about your behavior, I back her. We need to talk about you and Miss Cheyenne."

"Alright," Calen said, sticking his thumbs in the belt loops of his jeans, bracing himself for whatever was coming.

"When are you going to tell her you've imprinted?"

"I haven't," Calen insisted.

What? Ryne demanded.

"Speaking as your alpha, you definitely have."

Eh, Calen. I think he's right, Ryne admitted.

What do you mean, you think he's right? We can't have imprinted on her. Calen thought desperately. *She hates us!*

Well, I do feel different, and it certainly explains why you want to give up on her, but can't, Ryne reasoned.

Um, well. Calen thought, his mind going blank.

Say something! Ryne demanded.

"Well, fuck."

CHAPTER EIGHTEEN

CHEYENNE

*S*ophie was quiet on the way from the bake sale to Cheyenne's house.

"I'm sorry," Cheyenne said in the quiet. "I know I shouldn't have called you *my* omega, but I was so mad. The way he was looking at you? Ugh. He's so arrogant, it makes me want to slap that stupid smirk he has right off his face."

"I didn't mind," Sophie said quietly.

"Well, you should. He was just flirting with you to get a rise out of me, which I'm ashamed to say worked," Cheyenne said, shaking her head.

"No, I mean, I don't mind that you called me your omega," Sophie said, blushing.

Cheyenne stopped at the light and glanced over at Sophie, giving her a look.

"You don't?"

"No. I kinda thought that- well. I thought..." Sophie trailed off, blushing to the tips of her ears.

"What did you think?"

"I thought the same thing he thought, that when you said girls' night on the full moon that you meant..."

"You thought I meant we were having sex?" Cheyenne asked.

A brief honk from the vehicle behind her let her know that the light was green. She let off the brake and let their car surge forward.

"Sophie, I'm- I like men," Cheyenne said quietly.

"I know that I just thought… you really give off the energy of someone who likes both men and women."

"Do I?"

"Yeah, you really do."

"So, you thought we were going to- that we were having sex?"

"Well, yeah," Sophie said. "That's why I packed a bag. I thought when you said you wanted to try something different that you meant trying… me."

"Oh," Cheyenne said.

"I'm sorry, I made this really awkward," Sophie said.

"No, not at all. I hadn't considered it. I haven't ever been with a woman. I'm afraid I wouldn't be very good at it."

"You don't have to do anything," Sophie said. "Except kissing, which I'm sure you're really good at."

"I don't know," Cheyenne said.

"Look, you don't have to do anything. I'm just saying, if you want to experiment, you can be in charge."

"I wouldn't know what to do," Cheyenne fretted, now blushing herself.

"You don't have to *do* anything. You can just have me do things to you. You can just enjoy it, use me to… service you."

"That doesn't sound like fun for you,"

"Um, that's what's fun for me," Sophie said.

"You would like if I just- what? Laid there and told you what to do to me?"

"Yes," Sophie replied, her voice husky.

"Oh."

The two women sat in silence.

"I don't know that I would like it. I've only ever been with men before," Cheyenne confessed.

At that, Sophie flashed an uncharacteristically cocky grin.

"It may not be your thing, but trust me, if it is, I'll make sure you like it," she promised Cheyenne.

"So, your overnight bag wasn't just pajamas and stuff?"

"I mean, I have those, too, but mostly it's toys. I didn't know what you'd have, so I thought I would make sure we had options."

"Right,"

"Hey, we don't have to. We can have a movie night, or if it's awkward now, just drop me off at home."

"I think I want to," Cheyenne said. "But if it's not my thing, then-"

"Then we'll stop. I don't want to do something that isn't fun for you. I just want you to be happy. I know you'd rather be with a man tonight, but…"

"Oh god, Calen," Cheyenne groaned. "He's probably going to be hanging around."

"Technically, he's only allowed to make someone fight him if they're a male. The founding pack members who came up with the challenge rule didn't think a woman would dare challenge an alpha for the right to be in his chosen mate's bed. So, technically," Sophie grinned broadly, "all he can do is listen from the porch and wish he could come in."

"Heh, come in," Cheyenne chuckled.

Sophie laughed a little.

"Are you trying to convince me by reminding me that it'll make Mr. Cock Block as miserable and frustrated as he's made me?"

"Yes. Is it working?"

"Yeah, but if we're going to do this, we need to turn around," Cheyenne said, pulling off onto a side street to turn back toward the main part of town.

"What for?"

"Recovery snacks and drinks," Cheyenne said.

They were walking through the store when Cheyenne stopped.

"Oh, shit. I should maybe talk to Matt about this. He might mind."

Sophie chuckled and shook her head.

"Yeah, do that," Sophie said.

"Why do you say it like that?" Cheyenne asked, pausing with her phone in her hand.

"It was Matt who suggested you might need a little company since he's working," Sophie said. "But yeah, he'd probably appreciate the discussion."

"It's going to take some getting used to, having a boyfriend. It's weird after being single for so long. I sort of forgot he existed. Is that bad?"

> Cheyenne
>
> Hey, how's it going?
>
> Matt
>
> Busy, but good.
>
> If you're with Sophie, the answer is yes. Have fun.
>
> Cheyenne
>
> Well, that's direct.
>
> Matt
>
> You like direct.

Besides, I may not be able to text for a while and I want you to be able to have fun. If I can't be with you, I want you to have a good time.

Sophie is a good submissive, you'll like her.

> CHEYENNE
>
> *big eyes emoji*
>
> ... what if I hate it?
>
> MATT
>
> Then you will have taken the opportunity to try something new. Just communicate and be open about it.

You might not have been with a woman before, but you give off bi vibes like it's pride week.

MATT

Just relax and enjoy the experience.

Gotta run, got a call.

"So, do we want popsicles or ice cream?" Sophie asked, raising her eyebrow at Cheyenne when she looked up with a smile.

CHEYENNE LET Sophie unpack the groceries, which Sophie insisted on doing, while Cheyenne picked a movie for them to watch.

The movie was a romantic comedy. Sophie started off by sitting at Cheyenne's feet instead of on the couch, gently nudging her legs apart and grabbing her feet so she could take one of Cheyenne's feet in her lap and rub it with some oil that smelled divine.

"That feels so nice," Cheyenne moaned and Sophie beamed with pleasure.

The movie went on, and as the moon rose, Cheyenne's noises of pleasure at the foot rub were less platonic and more erotic. Sophie's hands moved up Cheyenne's legs, working her calves for a few minutes before turning around.

Cheyenne's wolf growled in pleasure at seeing Sophie kneeling in front of them, her hands on Cheyenne's legs.

"Such a good omega," Cheyenne praised. "Making me feel so nice."

"I can make you feel even nicer," Sophie offered, batting her eyelashes.

"Can you?" Cheyenne leaned forward, taking some of Sophie's bright red hair in her fingers and drawing her into a deep, lingering kiss that left them both breathless.

She might not have ever been with a woman before, but damn. Sophie's lips were impossibly soft, her mouth delicate and small.

Kissing someone like this was new to Cheyenne, as she had never been with a submissive man and no woman. She'd always been the one who was submissive to her lovers, or at least on equal footing. Being the one in charge was novel and gave her a heady rush. She wasn't entirely sure she loved it, but it was fun to try something new.

When the energy of the kiss began to wane, her mind scrambled, and then she decided to just lean into it and be the one in charge. She trusted Sophie to say something if it wasn't what she wanted, so Cheyenne reclined back, spreading her legs and giving Sophie a brief look. She didn't want to completely stop what they were doing to check in, but she didn't want her friend to feel anything but good about whatever they did.

Just because she was in charge didn't mean she didn't care about her feelings. Cheyenne knew of many girls who had been in Lillington's kitchen the morning after a full moon. They were either crying or shaken due to bio alphas going too far or too hard with omega pack members or susceptible humans under alpha magic.

Sophie's enthusiastic eyes sparkled as she asked, "What do you want me to do?"

"Use that mouth to show me just how good you can make me feel."

Cheyenne heard the distinct noise of a male wolf's whine outside her window and felt herself grow even more wet at the idea of Calen listening in to Sophie pleasuring her.

"You have an audience, so you better do a good job. I want him to hear how loud I can scream when I come apart," Cheyenne instructed.

Eagerly, Sophie knelt down, putting her face at the apex of Cheyenne's thighs, her eager tongue parting her.

"You smell so good," Sophie whispered reverently.

Before she could reply, Sophie's tongue found her clit and Cheyenne gasped, then moaned. She was right: Sophie did know how to make a woman feel good.

Sophie's eagerness and enthusiasm only grew with each bit of praise or encouragement. When her tongue slipped inside of Cheyenne's soaked cunt, Cheyenne cried out.

"Oh, moon, like that. Just like that, good girl, fuck me with your tongue," she moaned.

Sophie nodded and bobbed her head, sending her tongue in over and over. When it became too much, Cheyenne's hand found Sophie's hair, holding her there so her tongue was inside of her. Sophie fluttered her tongue, licking as deep as she could, making little noises as if Cheyenne's pleasure were her own.

When Cheyenne finally came, her cries of pleasure were echoed by the wolf outside her bedroom window in howls of frustration, or pleasure, she wasn't sure.

Sophie emerged, face triumphant and bright red, an enormous smile stretched across her face.

"Should I get some toys?"

Sophie had come prepared.

"I don't know what size you like, so I brought a variety," she explained, opening her bag of toys on Cheyenne's bed. Cheyenne blushed but picked out one that approximately matched the size of her favorite toy and handed it to Sophie.

Cheyenne nodded, anxiety blossoming.

"I know what I'm doing, you know," Sophie said with a quiet, gentle laugh.

"You do," muttered Cheyenne as her chest tightened.

"Hey, we can stop if you want. We can just have a movie night, and that would be okay."

Cheyenne felt sudden tears spring to her eyes, but before she could blink them away, they rolled down her cheeks, fat and hot.

"I'm just - really freaked out. What if I hate it and then it hurts your feelings and then we can't be friends anymore because I ruined it? Except I think it could be fun, but I don't really know, and I think part of the reason I liked it so much is because Calen could hear, which maybe makes me an awful person-"

Sophie cut off Cheyenne with a sudden hug.

"Oookay," she drawled, drawing out the word as she held Cheyenne around the middle, squeezing her in a comforting embrace.

They stood there until Cheyenne had calmed down and Sophie allowed her to straighten.

"That's a lot of feelings," Sophie said. "I don't hate you, I couldn't hate you, but while I would love to play, I don't think you're going to have fun. So, how about we take a bubble bath and then watch a movie and break out those snacks we got earlier?"

"But you brought toys," Cheyenne said, her face crumpling.

"And I got to give you an orgasm without toys, which you enjoyed. So I came to have fun with you, my *friend*. If I wanted some slutty person to have mindless sex with, I wouldn't be here. The only thing that will ruin this is you not having fun," Sophie said, putting her hands on both of Cheyenne's shoulders. "So, if it sounds good to you, let's take a bath, okay?"

"On one condition," Cheyenne said.

"Name it," Sophie said, eyes lighting up.

"We have snacks *in* the bath," Cheyenne said, her face splitting into a grin.

"Deal," Sophie said with a matching smile.

CHAPTER NINETEEN

CHEYENNE

*C*heyenne was running late. She and Sophie had stayed up entirely too late drinking and binge-watching heist movies. Sophie had been nice to Calen and brought him food and water, as he refused to leave his spot on the porch in wolf form. Cheyenne had rolled her eyes but said nothing as Sophie had made him a generous plate of cookies, fruit, and cheese. It wasn't like they hadn't gotten entirely too much food. Cheyenne just didn't want to encourage him.

"It's not like we're encouraging him. If anything, you're rewarding him for not bursting in when he heard you screaming earlier. I can only imagine how much self-control that took for someone who wants you for their mate."

Cheyenne had snorted and returned to the movie, not asking what Calen's wolf had done when Sophie had brought the snacks out for him. They'd fallen asleep on Cheyenne's couch, snuggled up under a pile of blankets, and it was only by the grace of the moon that Cheyenne had remembered to turn on her morning alarm the day before because otherwise, she could have easily slept until noon.

Leaving Sophie sleeping on the couch, Cheyenne had thrown on her work clothes, brushed her teeth hastily, and grabbed a handful of fruit on the way out the door. When she walked outside, dark clouds obscured the morning sky. Calen's wolf rose with an interrogative noise when she crossed the porch. She ignored him, rushed down the steps, and hurried to her car.

Putting her key in the ignition, the engine tried to turn over, but the car just wouldn't start. She tried several more times, checking her watch with desperation. Cheyenne sighed. She really didn't have time for this today. She was already running late, and she was supposed to be opening the shop today, as Shelby had a doctor's appointment. Calen's wolf padded to his truck, shifting, so he stood in his sweat-wicking clothes. He grabbed a pair of gym shorts, pulled them over the form-fitting spats he normally wore to jiujitsu to give a hint of modesty, and walked over.

Cheyenne opened her door and huffed as she sent a quick text, letting Ben know she would be a little late opening, but that everything was fine.

"Pop the hood," he instructed.

"No," she snapped, locking the doors as she got out.

"Cheyenne, I'm a mechanic. Let me take a look," Calen insisted.

"I don't need your help."

"Yes, that attitude is very admirable, except you literally do need a mechanic right now," Calen pointed out.

"I don't need *your* help, and you're not the only mechanic in town," she reminded him, keeping her phone out so she could text Bobby once she got rid of Calen.

A dramatic boom of thunder drew her attention and she sighed heavily.

"Fine, at least let me drive you to work."

"No! You're not my boyfriend. You're a stalker. Stalkers don't give their victims rides to work."

"I am not stalking you. I'm *courting* you, you bull-headed woman!" he snapped. "You're being ridiculous, you know that? You want me. You get so aroused around me that you can barely stand it. Why are you fighting this?"

"*I'm* being ridiculous? That's rich coming from the man who sleeps outside my door every night!"

"I wouldn't be sleeping outside if you'd let me inside, or stop trying to fuck other men. And also, yes, *you're* the ridiculous one here. You're denying yourself, and me, for no other reason than to spite me." Calen's jaw ticked, making the corded muscles of his neck stand out. "Besides, courting has been done this way for far more years than the modern idea of dating."

"It was also legal to buy and sell women for mates and wives for a long time. That doesn't make it the best, or ethical, way to do things," she pointed out.

Calen made a fist and brought his knuckles to his top lip, closing his eyes and looking like he was praying for patience.

"Just get in the truck, firecracker," he said, sounding tired.

"You don't take no well, do you?"

Cheyenne hoisted her bag on her shoulder and walked down her street; she was going to be late, but she didn't care. She was tired and horny and while that wasn't *exactly* his fault, it was close enough to the truth to let it stand for the moment.

Besides, his entire 'courting' campaign was infuriating, and she would not give him the satisfaction of letting him take care of her.

"And see, here I thought you weren't trying to get to know me." She swore she could hear the arrogant smirk he wore. It made her itch to slap it off his face. "Come on, Cheyenne, you're going to get soaked."

"I'd rather walk," she said primly.

She thought maybe he'd given up, but the jingle of his truck keys disabused her of that notion.

"You're going to be late."

"Yup."

"Cheyenne, let me give you a ride. It won't kill you."

"It might."

"You're so fucking stubborn," he rolled his eyes.

"You need a new line," she said.

"Will you *please* just get in the truck?" He asked, catching up to her.

"You know what? Yes. Yes, I will get in your truck when you admit that *this*," she gestured between the two of them. "Isn't inevitable between us."

She stood toe-to-toe with him, her chest brushing his, making her nipples tingle through her shirt. She met his gaze, her wolf's force of will pitted against his. Ryne's growl of challenge was so forceful that Cheyenne felt her whole body stiffen.

The conflict swirled in her. As an alpha, she couldn't stand the idea of him making a decision for her, deciding they were in a relationship, and not taking her no for an answer.

On the other hand, everything in her wanted to submit to him, to let him drag her into the house and let him force himself on her, holding her down and biting her neck while he forced his way between her legs. Cheyenne resisted the urge to curl her body against his, run her hands up his chest, and let him pull her into a rough kiss. She was about to break when he took a step back, giving her room to breathe the cool air that wasn't saturated with his scent.

"Enjoy your walk, firecracker," he breathed.

When Cheyenne started walking down the street, she could feel his eyes on her back and hear the rumble of his truck's engine inching down the road as she walked, and thunder boomed again overhead. She could have grabbed her umbrella, but she was already on the way and didn't want to make herself later than she already was going to be.

She didn't want someone to dictate her life to her, so why did she feel so disappointed? Her defiance didn't make her feel as satisfied as she'd thought it would. She thought he'd left when she heard someone honk and speed down the street.

As the rain came down in fat, cold droplets on the sidewalk, she peeked back and stopped cold. He wiggled his fingers at her, his face drawn in an expression she couldn't read, his one hand on the steering wheel. He leaned against the door, watching her as he inched down the road. With a roll of her eyes, she zipped up her jacket, shivering as she walked to work.

Not caring that he slowed traffic down, he followed her the entire way to her work, honking twice before pulling away.

CHAPTER TWENTY

CALEN

"ey man, what's up?" Owen asked, giving Calen a once-over as he walked into the day room in a dark mood.

"This woman, man," Calen grumbled, reaching in the fridge for an energy drink and an electrolyte-balancing drink, closing his eyes for a moment, hoping they would feel less like sandpaper when they opened.

When it had become clear that Cheyenne was going to stay up all night with Sophie, Scott had taken pity on him and brought him over a bottle of bourbon, which Calen had consumed all by himself, then transformed back into his wolf form to enjoy the cold full moon alone on her porch.

That was highly unpleasant, and so is this, Ryne thought into his mind as Calen's head pounded in time with his pulse.

"What's going on with Cheyenne now?"

"Same shit, different day."

"Well, if it's any consolation, you look fucking terrible and you smell like a distillery," Owen joked.

Calen silently cursed Owen for being happy and finding a girl he liked who liked him back.

I know I am supposed to be supportive or whatever, but this is getting ridiculous, Ryne thought irritably as Calen groaned when tones dropped for another truck over the radio.

"I wonder what it's like to be a human without a wolf in your head talking all the damn time," Calen mused.

"Boring," Owen offered Calen coffee, and Calen nodded gratefully. "So, what makes you keep at it?"

"Simple, life without wolves would be simple," Calen corrected.

Hey! I am a great wolf.

Imprinted, Calen said flatly.

I'm not convinced it was my fault. I don't even like her! Ryne snapped back.

"I can't just - not have her. I don't know. I mean, maybe I could. But something about her just won't let me see her with someone else until she's given me a chance," Calen said, popping the tab on his energy drink.

He wasn't going to tell anyone else about the imprinting. The only thing that first responders did better than handle an emergency was gossip, and the next thing he would know, Cheyenne would probably show up and key his truck for having the audacity to fall for her and forcing her and her wolf into a relationship she didn't want.

"She did give you a chance. You fucked it up. That full moon was your audition, and you blew it, man," Matt said smugly as he pulled a drink out of the fridge.

"You keep my mate's name out of your mouth, beta," Calen growled. "Fucking disrespectful little prick."

"Oh please, Merrick, as if you have any room to talk to me about how I talk about a woman. You can't get a girl unless you're scooping someone else's date."

He can't talk about her like that, Ryne thought with a warning growl.

"That's funny coming from the guy whose full moon 'date' was my sloppy seconds," Calen shrugged, trying to keep his temper, and Ryne's, under control.

"Man, you left her hanging. It wasn't my fault she would rather run out of your house without her socks than deal with you for one more round. I did make sure to leave the window open in case you wanted to jerk one off while you listened. She's like a fucking porn star when she *really* comes. I wanted to make sure you knew what it sounded like since you hadn't heard it before," Matt said with a smirk and a wink.

Oh, moon, no, he didn't just say that. Ryne snarled.

Calen launched himself across the room. The two went tumbling as fists flew. Patrick Lawson stood in the doorway, sighing heavily.

"It's too early for this shit," he muttered, then called loudly. "Chief!"

A few moments later, the chief was peering over Lawson's shoulder.

"Stupid pups," Jason grumbled. "It's too early for this shit- move over."

Stepping around Lawson, Jason inhaled deeply and bellowed.

"Oi! Have you lost your fucking minds?"

"No sir!" Matt said as he hauled back and got in one more punch.

"Alright, you, in my office." Jason pointed to Matt. "Owen, look at Merrick's eye."

Owen chuckled as he went to go grab an ice pack. "I'll get Ryder's student to do the evaluation. He could use the practice."

"Thanks," Calen said sarcastically, but Owen just grinned and shook his head.

"Owen! Did you see what happened?" Lawson stopped him on his way out to find the student.

"Uh, no sir. Didn't see a thing, I went temporarily blind in both eyes. Must be the imprinting," Owen said. "Come on, Merrick, let's get that eye looked at."

Calen grunted and made a rude gesture with his hand at Matt as he walked away. Matt lunged, but Patrick caught him neatly by the back of the shirt.

"Keep walking, beta. Calen, keep yourself together. This is a workplace, not a free-for-all. If you need to blow off steam, go to the gym, but keep it out of my building. I'm already going to have to write you up."

Calen nodded and trudged after Owen.

We need to get a handle on this, Ryne said.

Agreed, Calen said, thinking of Matt.

Not him. I mean Cheyenne! She's giving him attention that should only belong to us, and all you're doing is sitting around and moping. We need to tell her.

No. She has to come to want us on her own. No coercion. Telling her we imprinted obligates her to be with us, and I'm not fucking okay with that. End of discussion, Calen snapped at Ryne.

Alright, fine. But I'm just saying, you're wrong.

CHAPTER TWENTY-ONE

CHEYENNE

*T*hankfully, the rain stopped, so when work slowed down for the afternoon, Cheyenne was able to take a relatively dry walk down to the mechanic's shop a few blocks down on Main Street.

"Hey, Cheyenne!" The grease-covered mechanic smiled warmly.

"Hey, Bobby! I need your help. My car wouldn't start this morning. Can you look at it for me?"

"Nope," he responded, not taking his eyes off the screen as he typed on the ancient grime-covered keyboard with little plastic clicks.

"You're funny. Seriously."

"Seriously, I'm not getting in the middle of whatever alpha pissing match you and Merrick are having," the mechanic said, glancing up at her with an apologetic smile and a slight shrug.

"He called you?" Cheyenne demanded.

He was infuriating. She was gonna kill him... right after she got her car fixed.

"What do you think?" he said, giving her a steady look.

"You're picking his side by not helping me, you know that?"

"I'm not getting in the middle of you two."

"Will you at least order me a part?"

"Yeah. But I'm not touching your car."

"Okay. Fine."

STALKER

Let me know when you want me to drop by
and look at your car, firecracker.

CHEYENNE

Sorry, I can't give you the lengthy reply I want
to right now, my BOYFRIEND is picking me up
from Bobby's and taking me on a date.

STALKER

Mm-kay, well when your date is done, make
sure you let him know your future MATE is
going to be waiting on your front porch.

Bring me back some leftovers? *winking emoji*

Cheyenne took a moment to relieve the tenseness in her muscles, opening her jaw and blowing air out in a whoosh.

Matt answered her on the second ring.

"Well, hello beautiful," he greeted.

"Hi there," she greeted, trying to sound cheerful.

"What's wrong?" The sounds in the background were gone.

"Bobby won't look at my car," she said, taking a deep breath through her nose as angry tears sprung to her eyes.

It was one of the things that frustrated her most - the angrier she was, the more likely she was to cry. Although maybe she should let Bobby see her crying, it might earn her enough sympathy for him to look at her car. She rejected the idea. She had the internet, and if it wasn't too complicated, she could just do it herself. There were only so many reasons why her car wouldn't start, right?

"I'm sorry, baby. So, I guess that means you're ready for me to come pick you up," Matt said.

"I am if you don't mind."

"Not at all. I'll be there in fifteen."

Matt took her out for a lovely lunch at a little diner by the docks in Red River. The place was quiet except for three businessmen in suits who were briefly joined by a woman in a purple sundress and a floppy hat.

"Which one's daughter do you think she is?" Cheyenne asked in a whisper, nodding subtly to the only other occupied table.

"Oh, I think she's that short one's daughter. Only family can look at you with that level of casual loathing. Plus, they have the same nose."

"How can you see their noses from that far away?"

"I noticed when I went to the bathroom," Matt said with a laugh.

"Ooh, good idea!"

"Cheyenne, are you really going to the bathroom just to look at some strangers' noses?"

"No. I also want to look at her dress," Cheyenne said. "I love people watching and making up stories for people."

"Me too," Matt confessed with a little laugh. Spotting the waitress coming with their food, he said, "Hurry up and go snoop."

Cheyenne hurried past their table on the way back from the bathroom.

"Skylar," the older short round one said.

The woman replied something that Cheyenne didn't catch.

"Okay, so her name is Skylar. Isn't that a pretty name?"

"Yeah, you should add it to your list."

"My list?"

"Your list of baby names," he said.

"I don't have a list," she said, blinking in surprise. "Why would I have a list? I'm not pregnant yet."

She grabbed her fork and speared a piece of broccoli.

"Don't worry about it, I have one of the names you said you liked. I'll just add it to mine," Matt informed her, pulling his phone out for the first time.

"You have a list?" Cheyenne asked softly, eyes wide.

"Of course," Matt said, surprised. "I have a list of things we'll need for the baby too, so we don't forget to put them on the registry."

"Like what?" She asked.

"I'll tell you while you eat, so your food doesn't get cold," he said with a significant look at the bite she held suspended halfway between her plate and her mouth.

"You're- really all in, aren't you?" She asked.

"Of course I am," Matt said, with a confused smile. "I said I wanted to be your mate, and you aren't a good mate by ignoring what your mate wants and needs."

"Or by refusing to let a mechanic work on your mate's car," she added, thinking of Calen.

Hazel let out a sharp rebuke for talking about another man on their date with their actual potential mate, but Matt wasn't phased.

"Yeah, that's a dick move. Speaking of that, I have a friend who has a shop right down the street from here who can help you out," Matt said between bites of his grilled chicken. "He said if you get your car here he won't charge you labor."

"Thanks, but I'm going to see if I can just replace the battery. The internet says that it's either that or the alternator, most likely. If it's not the battery, we can check it out."

"Have you tried just jumping it?" Matt asked.

"Um," Cheyenne said, her cheeks coloring.

"When we get back, let's check that, and then I'll pick you up a battery if you really want to go that route. If you change your mind, we'll have them tow it up to Micah's shop."

"Thank you," she said. "If I don't have it fixed soon, I'll think about it," she promised. Taking another bite of her broccoli. "Thank you. I feel like we haven't had many real dates. Sorry, I'm kinda ruining the vibe with the car talk."

Matt set his chicken sandwich down with a stern look.

"Cheyenne, I know we haven't been doing this long, so let me explain this to you: I don't do things halfway. When I said I wanted to be your mate, I meant that I wanted to be the one to take care of you, to be the one you want to call when you have something go wrong, whether you need help or whether you just need someone to listen to you talk about it. Having a date where we can just deal with the mundane stuff that you would talk with me about isn't a letdown. It's a dream come true."

Before Cheyenne could respond, the waitress approached their table, her hand on her ample chest.

"That was so romantic. Honey, you keep that one forever. He's a good one. I swear if my boyfriend said anything like that, my panties would evaporate on the spot."

Cheyenne laughed and gave Matt a look. Matt colored slightly and mumbled something about just being honest and asked for the check.

"It's getting nasty. Looks like it's supposed to rain for the next three days."

"Damn."

"Well, I need an alternator."

"Have you had it tested?"

"No, but it wasn't the battery. The internet says it's probably the alternator, and since the only service I can get here is parts," she shrugged.

"I don't want you to waste your money."

"Then look at my car!" She said, tears of frustration pooling in her eyes.

"Please don't cry," he pleaded.

"Order me the stupid part then," she stormed out.

Bobby looked after her and picked up the phone.

"Merrick, it's Bobby. Look, Cheyenne was just here trying to order an alternator, but she's got no fucking clue what's actually wrong with it. Go fix her car or I am. This is ridiculous. She doesn't have the money to blow on car parts she might not need."

Cheyenne was in the middle of discussing the new ad they were running, featuring a few pictures of Cheyenne and a particularly artistic arrangement she'd made a few days prior.

"Cheyenne!" a loud voice called from the front of the store.

"Yes?" she said, poking her head out of the kitchen, smiling when she saw Scott. "Oh, hey Scott. You here for your arrangement?"

"Gimme your keys," Scott said.

"What?"

"Give me your keys. I'm fixing your car," Scott insisted, holding out his hand with an impatient raise of his eyebrows.

"Oh my god. You're the best, thank you! I could kiss you. One sec. Thank you, THANK YOU!" She disappeared into the kitchen and reappeared a few minutes later, throwing her arms around the deputy, who grunted.

"Mm-hmm." He said gruffly. "I want a discount on my arrangement."

"You got it!"

Her phone buzzed just before she had to leave for the day.

SCOTT

Your keys are inside on the kitchen table. Car's fixed.

CHEYENNE

Was it the alternator? How much do I owe you?

SCOTT

It was a spark plug wire, a three-minute fix.

You don't owe me anything. This is just what neighbors do.

CHEYENNE

I do owe you. Thank you!!!

SCOTT

Seriously, you don't owe me a thing.

You want a ride home?

CHEYENNE

Actually, that would be great.

CHAPTER TWENTY-TWO

CALEN

Calen put away the tools he had brought but hadn't needed, in the back seat of his truck, wiping his hands on his greasy pants out of habit. She wouldn't know that he'd fixed her car, but she would have something safe to drive when the bad weather came in over the next few days.

The fact that she'd spent days walking to work instead of just letting him take care of her hurt, even though he knew it wasn't fair or reasonable to expect her to show him anything other than animosity with the situation between her, him, and Matt.

Ryne didn't suggest that they should tell her anymore, but Calen could feel his frustration that simmered along with Calen's own at the fact that she was their mate, and clearly didn't feel the mating bond like they did.

"You sure you don't want me to tell her you fixed it?" Scott asked when Calen shut the back door on the side of the truck he now thought of as Cheyenne's side, even though she'd never been anywhere close to riding in his passenger seat.

The thought of her riding passenger princess, her hand held fast in his across the console, made his heart beat faster. He wanted her, and even though he wanted her sexually, it was more than that. He wanted little ordinary everyday moments like doing a quick fix for her car to be the new normal for them. A little teasing and playful harassing would be fine. He loved how fiery she was, but he wanted the happy, nice, joyful parts of her, too. Fuck Matt Griffith for getting those moments when he wasn't.

"Nope. She'd probably stop driving it out of spite," Calen said with a grin and a shake of his head. At least his woman was stubborn. She would need it living with an alpha wolf.

She wouldn't refuse to drive it if you fucked her into submission, Ryne pointed out.

As soon as she consents, I will, Calen thought back irritably.

"You two have a weird relationship," Scott said as he shook his head.

"You're telling me," Calen sighed.

Scott's phone pinged, and he glanced at it, tensing slightly and giving Calen a look.

"Eh, actually, it looks like she did want that ride home. You're not gonna hit me or anything, are you?" Scott glanced at Calen with a look of wary concern.

"Are you going to try anything?" Calen asked, raising an eyebrow.

Scott's reply was a nonplussed glare, and Calen shrugged, rolling his shoulders to ease the tension there. At least his time in the gym was paying off, but between the tension caused by his imprinting and his near-constant muscle soreness from lifting, his muscles were always in need of a good stretch.

"Then no, I won't hit you," he told Scott.

"Alright, well, I'll grab her and then I'll take her home."

"Thanks for your help," Calen said, glad he'd been able to fix her car for her, ignoring the fact that she hadn't really let him do it, and the sharp stab of hurt it caused that their mate hadn't let them do even one simple, nice thing for her.

CHAPTER TWENTY-THREE

CALEN

EIGHT MONTHS LATER

"*H*ey, Griffith," Calen said, walking into the ambulance bay to ask Matt and his partner to switch trucks so he could service theirs.

"Stay out of my fucking way, Merrick," Matt said tersely, shouldering past Calen.

"I was going to say I needed your truck," Calen snapped, eyes narrowing.

"Oh. I thought you'd be gloating. Sorry," Matt said.

Calen racked his brain, trying to think about what he could have to gloat about. He could count less than a dozen times Cheyenne had deigned to have a conversation with him over the last eight months. Every single one of them had included her shouting, or at least snarling at him to leave her alone.

She'd taken to masturbating loudly during every full moon, making as much noise as possible while he sat outside in his wolf or human form and alternately strained to hear every sound, or tried to block it out when her noises made it impossible for him to do anything but think of her and how her body would feel if he was the one making her make those sounds.

Matt had stopped trying to come around on the full moon at the chief's insistence after one fight, which had left Calen and Matt so bloody and bruised that they'd both been unable to work the next day. Calen was fairly certain that more than once Matt had been on the other end of a video call when Cheyenne enjoyed her new full moon self-pleasure routine, but Calen preferred not to think about that.

"I don't know what you're talking about," Calen said, shaking his head.

If anything, Matt, who had been on a date with Cheyenne last night until almost midnight, should be the one bragging. She'd come home reeking of Matt's scent, and when Calen had greeted her from what had become his corner of her porch, she'd lost her mind.

Her shouts that she was tired of him ruining her night every single night just by being there had been especially sharp and cutting, and Calen imagined that the contrast of coming home to the man she didn't want on her porch after the date with the man she did want was making her irritable. The drink she'd thrown at him had left his skin sticky. She had looked embarrassed but hadn't apologized when Scott had come outside to see what the commotion was. His mate had stormed into the house, while Calen had stood there, then stooped to pick up the soda cup from her dinner with Matt, walked over to the trash cans on the side of the street, and placed the cup inside with a heavy sigh.

No, Calen had no bragging rights that day, but Matt was looking at him with a death glare.

"Do you know something I don't?"

Matt shook his head, glared at Calen, and said that he would grab his stuff off the truck so Calen could have it.

"Matt, look, I'm sorry, alright? I know this whole thing between us with Cheyenne..." Calen trailed off, genuinely feeling bad for him.

Matt was a good man, and even though Calen wanted to hit him most of the time for being the man Cheyenne wanted, he had taken excellent care of Calen's mate, and for that Calen could be perversely grateful. If she wouldn't let Calen take care of her, he wanted someone to do it.

"Look, Calen, I really don't give a shit about anything you have to say," Matt broke in. "Cheyenne is a good girl, and-"

"I imprinted on her." The words blurted out without Calen having any intention of him saying them.

"You- really?"

"Yeah, that's why I can't just - let her be."

Matt stared at Calen for a beat, then another, then he nodded.

"Makes sense, I guess. You haven't told her because…"

"Because I wanted her to choose me willingly. Without any outside obligations. I just couldn't let you have her because…" Calen shrugged, unwilling to say the words to Matt first.

"Because she's your mate," Matt supplied.

Well, I supposed the wolf's out of the den now, Ryne thought.

It's time. I don't want to keep doing this with her.

"Well, we broke up," Matt said, looking away. "Good luck, I guess. You may want to tell her, though. I'm pretty sure she's still considering the Lawson's as fathers, since they're captains and a little less… beta than me about their partners."

Matt's color deepened, and he looked away. Calen stuck his hand out.

"You know, later on, when things aren't so fresh, maybe one day we could go grab a beer after work," Calen suggested.

Matt took the preferred hand, shaking it.

"Maybe. Not today though," he said with a little chuckle.

"Not today," Calen agreed as they let their hands fall away.

No, today he was going to go claim his mate, and hopefully she would say yes.

CHAPTER TWENTY-FOUR

CHEYENNE

"*E*ight months. Eight months he's been cock blocking me and it's making me crazy! Do you know how long it's been since I had sex?" Cheyenne said as she aggressively chopped the carrots for Ma in the kitchen at Lillington's.

"Eight months?" Sophie guessed.

"Well, like six months, but close enough! I had to get a recharge-able toy because I was running out of batteries! That's ridiculous. I'm an alpha female. I could have my pick of males to mate with, but oh no, Calen and his stupid courting…" she continued under her breath as she chopped the carrots with such vigor, that some pieces flew to the floor. "Matt broke up with me last night because of him because it was just too stressful for him to be with someone with an alphahole-stalker making a real relationship impossible."

"Hey! Watch it," Ma called.

"Wow."

"Mm-hmm. I may kill him."

"You could fuck him and then kill him once he falls asleep," someone suggested.

"I'm not giving him the satisfaction of winning," Cheyenne said with venom.

"I don't get it. You like alphas, right?" Emma asked from her perch in the corner. "Why not just... give him a second chance to prove himself and move on? I mean, most guys aren't this kind of persistent, and there's something to be said for that."

"You're one to talk!" Another girl laughed. "You and Ryder were tiptoeing around each other for months before you finally figured your shit out."

"Yeah, but half the time, Ryder didn't know if he was coming or going. We were 'just friends' - then he'd be super possessive and jealous. It was like dating Dr. Jekyll and Mr. Hyde."

"Plus, she had James. Just his voice with that accent is enough to make any girl second-guess her commitment to her man," Ma said from the door.

"Forget his voice! His abs are where it's at," another girl laughed.

"Nope, his best asset is definitely his mouth," Emma grinned. "He eats pussy like it's an Olympic sport, and he's *very* competitive."

"What about that guy who's living in that apartment in the community center?"

Emma was a sound mage who had a sound studio and worked part-time facilitating community events.

Recently, a handsome stranger had moved into town and taken the apartment above the community center. The entire town, particularly the female population.

"Alec?" Emma asked. Cheyenne paused as she peeled more carrots into a large stockpot. "I wouldn't know."

"Has he been with anyone since he's come to town?" someone asked.

"Not that I know of," Emma said, flushing deeply. "Hang on, let's not get off track. So, what would Calen have to do to get you to stop fighting him? Because if I had a man who was handsome and dedicated to courting me, I wouldn't be holding out."

"That's why you're not an alpha shifter," one of the girls teased Emma.

"I don't know. I guess I want him to stop treating me like it's a foregone conclusion that I'm going to give in to him."

"He's an alpha. I don't know that they know any other way to be. Besides, weren't you saying you didn't want a man who gave in to you, a man who took charge?" Sophie.

"Whose side are you on?" Cheyenne chucked a carrot at her. Sophie tried to catch it, but it bounced off her fingertips and would have hit the waitress in the face when she popped her face in.

"I'm on the side of orgasms!" Sophie said.

"Amen to that. Cheyenne, stop throwing carrots," Ma instructed. "Emma, James is here looking for you."

"Speaking of orgasms," someone said, Emma laughed and waved.

"Get some for me!" Cheyenne called.

"I will!" Emma called over her shoulder as she left.

"So, are you really gonna keep holding out?" Sophie asked, bumping Cheyenne's shoulder.

"I don't know," Cheyenne said. "I don't like letting him win."

"You accepting him on your terms and letting him blow your mind is not losing, honey," Ma said, taking a seat with a cup of tea. "Take it from someone who's seen a lot of young men go after a woman, you're irritated because he's doing exactly what you want an alpha to do - taking charge and sticking to his guns."

"Well," Cheyenne hedged.

"Give him another chance. At this point, it's all your ego anyway. The worst thing that happens is you don't spend the full moon alone. Use protection, but let him fuck your brains out and enjoy it. Give your lady town a vacation after your dry spell."

She was on the way home from Lillington's when her phone rang.

"Hello?"

Brian Lawson's voice came from the other end of the line. "Hey, Cheyenne! How are you?"

"I'm great. How are you, Brian?"

"I'm wonderful. Listen, I need a favor."

"Okay, what's up?" Cheyenne asked.

"Can you swing by?"

"Yeah, I'm in the car right now, in fact. Is everything okay?"

"Oh yeah, Pat has a new sourdough starter recipe and I have a cold, so I can barely taste anything. I need a taste tester since my congestion renders my taste buds useless for my husband.

"Ooh, say less. I'll be there in two shakes of a wolf's tail."

Cheyenne ended up spending far more of her afternoon than she thought she would sampling breads, giving Patrick feedback on the taste, texture, and smell of a variety of breads, letting Patrick insist that she try them with different spreads and toppings to see how they changed the flavor. Brian sat in the living room with a bowl of fresh-made chicken soup and an endless stream of hot tea made lovingly by his mate, while Cheyenne filled up on sample after sample of bread.

When she finally insisted she couldn't eat another bite, Patrick thanked her profusely, sending her home with a container of chicken soup for herself and a loaf of bread as a thank you.

"I have a baking competition and since *someone*," he gave his mate a significant look. "Decided to get sick. I needed a sub."

"I'm not sure how much help I actually was, but I enjoyed it," Cheyenne said. Patrick opened the front door, seeing that it was raining. He frowned.

"Let me walk you out. It's slick," Patrick said, putting a hand on the small of her back.

"Thank you. I can barely waddle," she said. "You're going to ruin my figure with all that."

Patrick laughed, giving her a once-over. "That's the greatest compliment a woman as lovely as you can give someone like me, so thank you. You drive safe, and enjoy that soup."

"I may end up having it tomorrow. I can barely walk, much less think about doing anything other than passing out on the couch when I get home."

She managed to get home, and for the first night in months, Calen wasn't there. Instead of feeling relief, she had a little pang of something like sadness. Had she finally gotten used to him being around all the time?

Maybe Ma and the girls at the diner were right, and she should give him another chance. The worst-case scenario was that she let him into her bed and he didn't bring his alpha energy- again. Then she had an idea, one that had her moving off the couch and to her bedroom, sorting through her lingerie.

"Don't you have anything better to do?" Cheyenne asked in a teasing tone as she opened the door, cocking her hip out tantalizingly, her stomach fluttering with nervous butterflies.

She felt her nipples pucker under her lingerie. Instead of the witty retort she was hoping for so she could invite him in, he phased, eyes blazing with rage.

"Oh yeah, because this is my idea of a great way to spend my night off!" He shouted, taking her aback. "Freezing my ass off because the woman I imprinted on won't stop trying to fuck other guys, including coworkers who I used to like working with, and now my captains. No, Cheyenne, apparently I don't have anything better to do than sit on your fucking porch."

Cheyenne opened her mouth, but he wasn't done. His face purple with rage, he started pulling on the clothes he'd left in a neat, folded pile on her front porch beside the railing.

"Oh, and I *love* when you play with yourself so I can hear it and can't fucking do anything unless I want to break down the door and violate you. That's pretty high on my list, too. But you know what my top favorite thing is?" He asked, drawing menacingly close, zipping up the zipper of his uniform pants.

She shook her head, unable to find the words to reply, shocked by his aggressive tone and demeanor... and did he say he'd imprinted? And what was he talking about, saying she was sleeping with his captains? She'd gone over to the Lawson's to eat bread, for the moon's sake!

"My absolutely favorite is when the woman I'm head over heels in love with bitches to anyone who will listen at Lillington's because all I want in the world is to be close to her, even if it means my wolf and I sit around outside on her porch like a simp while she pretends I don't even exist." Cheyenne tried to open her mouth, to explain why she'd been at the Lawsons, to apologize for how she'd acted, but he continued, months of repressed frustration all spewing out at once. "Yes, believe me, Cheyenne, I *wish* I had better things to do than try to win a woman who is a selfish bitch and won't give me a chance because she's too stubborn to know what's good for her! Close your godsdamned door. It's too cold to be outside in that... outfit."

She stood, hand on the door handle, too stunned to move. He huffed, stepping forward. She jumped back, afraid of what he was going to do. He grabbed the door handle, slamming it shut. She covered her hand with her mouth, stifling her sobs as she started to cry.

She started when he hammered on the door.

"Lock your door, mate!" He bellowed.

She turned the deadbolt with shaking hands, then put her back to it, sliding down to the floor, crying.

She couldn't even be mad. Everything he'd said was true. She'd been stubborn, she'd hurt him, and she deserved every bit of his anger. She looked at the candles she'd lit around the room, rising to blow them out.

Grabbing her phone, she left the food on the table and went to bed. She checked her phone every few minutes, but no goodnight text came. He'd given up on her, and she couldn't even be mad. As her stomach ache grew, she cursed herself for being such an idiot. She shouldn't have eaten so much stupid bread. She shouldn't have tried to make things right with Calen, or maybe she should have given him a second chance months ago. She cried until her tears soaked the pillow, and still her stomach ache grew.

This sucked.

CHAPTER TWENTY-FIVE

CALEN

*A*fter he'd driven past the Lawson's, stopped at the stop sign, and overheard the conversation between Cheyenne and Patrick, he'd lost his mind. Throwing his phone, he'd gone home to his apartment and showered, livid that she'd jumped right from being in a relationship with Matt to fucking the Lawsons without even having a conversation with him.

This is what happens when you don't have important conversations, Ryne had told him.

Yeah, I fucking know! Calen had shouted at his wolf. *Now she could be pregnant with someone else's baby and it's all my fucking fault. Don't you think I know that?*

Then he'd been even more stupid and gone to her house before he'd calmed down, thinking that being near her would calm him. Instead of calming him down, the sight of her in lingerie with her stupid, flirtatious smile had sent him over the edge. The thought of her teasing him when she'd clearly been with at least one other man that day who was trying to get her pregnant had him in a blind rage that he couldn't control any more than he'd controlled his imprinting on her.

He'd yelled at her and told her in the worst possible way about his imprinting, then left her alone. The fear in her eyes when he reached to close her door cut him to the core. He'd not only yelled at her, he'd scared her. He'd worked in near-silence with Ryder as his partner, jumping in on a shift that was already staffed just to give him something to do besides sit at home and stew, or worse, go back to Cheyenne's porch and say more things he would have to apologize for because his temper was hot.

He'd worked all night and had spent a small fortune buying a new phone from a cell phone store that was open all night in Red River after their last transport to Mountain Regional Hospital. He'd just activated the phone to get calls and texts when tones dropped and his radio went off.

Communications to Medical Base. Standby for traffic. 149 Franklin Avenue, reference altered mental state.

"Medic 20 en route," Medic twenty's paramedic responded from the room next door to Calen's, Owen's voice carrying through the paper-thin walls.

Calen racked his brain. 149 Franklin. Who lived at 149 Franklin? Then he growled. He'd seen the numbers 149 every day for almost an entire year, and he'd almost missed it. 149 Franklin was his mate's address.

He barreled down the hallway, throwing open Ryder's door without so much as a knock.

"Ryder! Get in the truck," Calen

"Twenty's got it," Ryder said, yawning and giving Calen a sleepy and slightly mutinous look that implied he wasn't going anywhere.

"That's Cheyenne's address," Calen snapped.

"Aw hell," Ryder said, rolling out of his bunk.

Calen pulled out his phone, five missed calls and a few texts, all from Cheyenne.

CHEYENNE

11:46 pm Hey. I'm sorry about tonight. Can we talk later?

12:23 am I really am sorry.

4:19 am I know you're mad at me, but I'm really sick.

6:36 am Please come back.

"Fuck," Calen cursed.

Ryder somehow beat him to the driver's door, telling dispatch they were on the way and shouting an explanation to Owen and his partner as he and Calen loaded up.

Calen tried to call her back, but she didn't answer. She didn't answer the door, so he walked around to the back, picking up her spare key from the container in a flowerpot and letting himself in, much to the chagrin of the firefighter who was ready to break down the door.

"Cheyenne? Baby, answer me!"

He found her in the bathroom, wearing nothing but a pair of underwear. A t-shirt was crumpled on the floor, covered in sick.

Ryne reminded them that if he hadn't thrown his phone, they could have been there sooner, but Calen snarled at him to shut up so they could take care of their mate.

"Oh, baby," he said. Turning, he instructed the firefighter who had followed him in. "Hey, grab me a sheet."

"Cheyenne, tell me what's wrong. Are you hurting?" He noted her pallor and the sheen of sweat clinically as Ryder made his way around him, perching himself on the edge of the tub.

Someone handed him a sheet. The scent calmed him, a mix of her laundry soap and her own scent. He draped it over her.

"Ryder is gonna check you out, okay? Where does it hurt? Put a finger on it."

She barely touched her right lower abdomen, between her belly button and her hip, her movements slow and guarded.

"When did it start?"

"Yesterday. I didn't feel very good, but I thought it was just because I was upset and I ate too much," she grimaced.

"Did the pain start there, or did it move?"

"It started here." She touched near her belly button.

"Merrick, BP's a little low." Ryder's voice was exceedingly calm, casual and light, his eyes meeting Calen's with the slightest tilt of his head.

"How low?"

"Eighty-six over forty," Ryder said, his eyes meeting Calen's.

Shit, they needed to transport her right fucking now, Ryne growled.

"That's not right," she slurred, frowning a little as she swayed slightly.

"Okay, let's get a stretcher in here," Calen called.

"That's the wrong numbers," she mumbled. "That's bad, right?"

"He's not very good at this, he probably got it wrong," Calen lied smoothly, not wanting to worry her more than he needed to. "I'll check you again in the truck, okay? So we're going to get you there, we're going to move you. Ready?"

"No! No!" she shouted, "Don't touch me. Don't. I'll move myself."

"We can do it fast," Calen offered.

"Don't. I'll do it." Her whole body shook as she climbed onto the stretcher, her face growing pale as he watched.

"You drive," Ryder said.

"Like hell," Calen began.

"Look, I've been where you are. I'll take care of her like it's Emma on the stretcher, but you can't be back there in my way. Don't make a scene or I'll have a volunteer drive the truck and you can take your POV."

"Fine," Calen said. "But you better treat her like it's Emma, or I swear to the moon goddess..."

"Yeah, I know," Ryder said as they moved the gurney through the house and out the front door.

CHAPTER TWENTY-SIX

CHEYENNE

*C*heyenne opened her eyes in a hospital recovery room, blinking slowly to clear her vision. Calen was sitting in the chair next to her, elbows resting on his knees, his fingers laced through his hair. She wanted him to look up, to say something nice to her. Then she remembered what he'd said the last time they'd talked and she had to try to fix it.

"Hi," she croaked.

"Hey," his head popped up, his eyes looking at her, then the monitors and back to her face. "How are you feeling?"

"I'm sorry," she slurred. He tried to stop her but her words poured out, "I was selfish, and I knew I hurt your feelings. Everything you said was true and I'm sorry. I know you hate me, but I want to take it back, but I know it's too late, but-"

"Cheyenne," he said, putting a finger to her lips. "It's not too late. I want to talk about this, but right now I need you to know what happened. Your appendix burst, you had emergency surgery to remove it and clean out the infection."

"That explains why I felt so awful," she said, grimacing at the memory.

"Yeah. But you're doing okay now."

"I feel wooshy," she said, wrinkling her nose in disgust as the room spun.

"That's the drugs," Calen informed her, putting a hand on hers.

"I don't like it," she blinked slowly and shook her head as she tried to clear it, causing the world to tilt alarmingly, so she closed them again and held still.

"It's better than being in pain. Also, you can't phase until your stitches are out."

"I hurt, but this is nothing like it was before," she said, making him grimace.

"I'm sorry I didn't see your calls or texts," he said, his face clouding with guilt.

"I understand. I wouldn't have answered me either," she ducked her head, eyes filling with tears. "Sorry, I don't know why I can't stop crying. I'm not mad or anything."

"Some people do that after they wake up from anesthesia, it's normal. Also, when your mate is an asshat, I'm told crying is normal. And I wasn't ignoring you - I broke my phone. I had to get a replacement. I had no idea you'd called until the call came out over the radio."

"You weren't just mad?" she asked, biting her lip, more tears spilling over.

His wolf growled that he would rather see her mad at them than crying.

You should boss her around or something, his wolf suggested.

"I was mad, but you should know one little spat isn't enough to run me off." He grinned. "I was fully ready to come back and fight some more when I got off work."

"Maybe eight months' worth was enough to change your mind," she shrugged, her gaze watery,

"No, baby. I'm in this for the long-haul."

The nurse came in and bustled about the room.

CHEYENNE WAS SENT HOME two days after her surgery. Her mate, the phrase still seemed strange, only left her once in the middle of the night, reappearing in the morning without an explanation. Instead of his truck, he had her car. When she gave him a confused look, he shrugged.

"I thought this would be easier for you to get in and out of." He explained. "I should have asked."

"No, it's great. Thank you for taking me home." Her face fell. "Oh, it's probably disgusting."

"It's not. I made sure it was cleaned up," he assured.

"You didn't have to do that."

"Stop arguing with me trying to take care of you," he grumbled.

"Old habits," she said with a chuckle. "Hey, you missed the exit."

"I'm taking you to my house," Calen informed her

"I want to go home," she said, sighing in tired frustration.

Calen didn't answer, just glanced sideways with a stubborn set to his mouth.

"I'm not being stubborn, all my stuff is there. Let me get some stuff at least."

"I'll go back and grab anything you need. You need to get some rest," Calen insisted, leaving his left hand on the steering wheel and grabbing her hand with his.

WHEN SHE CAME IN, she noticed little changes in his apartment since the one night she'd been there.

"Oh, Calen," she breathed.

He'd redecorated his bedroom. The bed spread she'd fingered longingly at the mall with a friend one afternoon was on the bed, coordinated throw pillows littered the surface. A bed food tray sat at the foot of the bed on top of a steamer trunk.

The closet door was open, laundry overflowing from the hamper beside its open door.

"You want to change?" He asked.

"I want to shower first."

"Okay. Sit down while I get the water going."

She was shy about removing her clothes.

"I'm okay, you can go," she said, biting her lip.

"I'm not leaving this room. I don't have to join you in there if you don't want me to, but I need to know you're alright." When she blushed, he reminded her, "I've seen you naked before, mate."

"But I don't want to tease you," she said, her face crumpling at the memory of his reaction to her in lingerie. Would seeing her naked make him mad all over again if he couldn't have sex with her now because of her stitches?

Besides that, she hadn't really processed the fact that he'd imprinted on her, and she needed a little time to adjust to he idea.

"I can handle it," Calen assured with a smile.

Stripping out of her shirt, she let it fall to the floor, he twirled his finger, indicating that she should turn around and he unclipped her bra for her. Shimmying out of her pants and underwear, she didn't look at him, testing the water. Climbing in, she let out a long sigh of bliss.

"If you start to feel overtired, tell me."

"Mm-hmm," she replied, massaging shampoo into her scalp.

She almost didn't admit it, but after washing and conditioning her hair, she squirted soap on a cloth, staring down at it. She was beyond tired. Closing her eyes, she took a steadying breath.

"Calen?"

"You tired?"

"Yeah, but I've only done my hair." He had to have already been naked, because he stepped into the shower behind her, taking the cloth from her hand gently.

"Thank you," she whispered.

"Mm-hmm."

He was careful with her, his hands moving over her skin with gentle and professional efficiency. He made no comments and his hands didn't linger anywhere, his expression neutral except when they met eyes and he gave her a gentle smile.

"All done," he said when he'd washed her all over. "Let's get you in bed."

"Can we just stand here for a minute? The water feels so good."

"One minute," he conceded.

She curled against his chest, nuzzling him. She couldn't shift into her wolf form until her stitches were removed, but Hazel was restless, itching to be let out.

"When you get your stitches out, I'll take you up the mountain for a run, just the two of us," he promised as if he could sense her thoughts.

"I hate this," she sighed.

"Yeah, I've had stitches, it sucks," he agreed.

He got her back to the bedroom, although she insisted on walking herself.

"Right side of the closet," he said. "I'll be right back."

There were clothes, women's clothes, almost completely filling the right half of the closet. An entire wardrobe, minus the bras. She selected a tunic and a pair of underwear, not wanting to bother with pants.

"You like them? Oh- wow." He swallowed, eyes traveling over her as he licked his lips.

"Sorry, I'll put some pants on."

"Don't. I love looking at you."

He tore his eyes away, looking at her face. "I have to work this week, but I would really appreciate it if you stayed here, for a little bit at least. You can go back to the other house if you want, but I'm asking nicely."

"You didn't say please." She said in a soft, playful testing tone. His hungry look returned, and he prowled across the room, standing straight, his dominant aura challenging hers.

Not breaking eye contact, he leaned down, in a tone that sounded like a command, not a plea, he said, "Please, stay."

"So bossy," she dropped her eyes, giving in to him. "But, since you asked so nicely."

"Get in my bed," he commanded softly, not lacing it with any of his authority.

"Yes, sir," she said quietly, eyes sparkling as she saw his pupils dilate. She climbed into bed, and he left and brought her back a tray of food with a full water bottle.

"I have to go in to work. My phone is on, do you have the number to call the base directly?"

"No." He reached for her phone, adding him to the top of her contacts, the base second, and removing Matt entirely.

"There you go. Call me if you want or need anything. Anything at all."

"Okay."

"The fridge should have enough food, but if there's something you want, have it delivered. Here's my card," He pulled out his wallet.

"I have money, I'm not taking your card," Cheyenne said, pursing her lips.

"Please?" He asked.

"No thank you."

"Fine. I'm going to be late. Be good and rest, alright?"

"I will," she promised.

He looked like he wanted to say something. He stood there for a moment awkwardly, then nodded and left without another word, leaving her to bask in his scent and think about what life would be like if she accepted his claim and this was *their* apartment, instead of his.

CHAPTER TWENTY-SEVEN

CALEN

*T*hey spent an easy week together. He didn't try to have sex with her, not that he didn't want to. He did, however, make every attempt to move her in permanently. She respectfully, but firmly, resisted him at every turn. The only fight they had was when she insisted on sleeping on the couch after he'd had a long shift.

"Cheyenne- you just had surgery. You are not sleeping on the couch," he'd said with an edge to his voice.

"Fine. Then I'm going back home," she retorted.

"Why are you so stubborn?" Calen had demanded, alarmed at the thought of her leaving his apartment.

What if she changed her mind when she got home? He'd gotten used to her scent in his bed, to her being in his space. The thought of going back to sleeping on her porch made him sick when they'd come so far in the last week.

"Because I'm horny and I want to have sex so bad I can't see straight, but I can't have any sex until my stitches are out, and that isn't for two more days!"

Her cheeks shone red against her pale skin, her pupils dilated, and her body fairly shaking with need. He stepped closer and inhaled deeply, Ryne growling with need at her nearness and her arousal.

"Take off your shirt," Calen ordered.

"No!"

"Not like that. I want to see your stitches." He gestured for her to come to him, kneeling in front of her.

Lifting her shirt, he inspected them closely, pressing near the incision.

"This is healed fine. I can take them out for you."

"I don't want you to get in trouble."

"You're adorable. Lay down on the bed, I'll be right back."

He came back with his jump kit, pulling out some small scissors, alcohol pads, and sterile strips.

"It won't hurt?" She asked with a half-step back.

"It may pull a little bit, I promise it won't hurt too much."

"Okay." She looked so scared and vulnerable, he couldn't help but lean down and take one finger under her chin, offering her a gentle kiss of reassurance.

"Let's get this taken care of," he said as his body buzzed with need to have her.

He pulled on gloves, sterilized his tools and snipped her stitches, placing a few sterile strips over the spot.

"All done."

"Thank you."

"Of course," he smiled kindly, cleaning up.

"Would you help me with... the other thing?" She asked.

"Which other thing?" He asked, his professional demeanor changing when he noticed how she looked at him, breathing fast, pulse beating rapidly. "Oh, I would love to give you orgasms, but I'm not having sex with you until you're ready to accept me as your mate. I can't do this with you if you aren't all in."

"I want to be ready," she said, biting her lip anxiously.

"It's okay that you aren't," he said. "I just can't have your body if I can't have all of you. I wouldn't be okay."

Ryne chuffed in approval at Calen's communication. *It's about time we started talking to her about your feelings.*

"I'm sorry," she said, her expression pained.

147

"Don't be sorry. You're perfect. It's okay to take time."

"It's scary," she confessed.

"Yeah, I know."

"So," he grinned, hooking a finger into her waistband, pulling it down as he planted kisses along her hipbone and down her thigh. "I won't fuck you, but I'll take care of you."

TWENTY MINUTES LATER, she was screaming his name with his face buried between her legs, fingers buried deep inside of her pussy.

"Calen. I want to fuck you. I want you."

"No," he said, as he fluttered his fingers inside of her.

"Please, please," her fingers dug into his arm, her eyes blazing with need.

"No, baby," he made her come again with his fingers. She lay on the bed, shaking.

"You're mean," she said, panting.

"*That* was mean?" he asked, incredulous.

"Yes, absolutely."

"If that's mean, just imagine how good it'll be when I'm nice," Calen said with a suggestive grin.

"Oh god. You hush," she commanded, rolling over on her stomach.

"Mm-hmm. I could have you bent over the kitchen counter, on the couch, in the truck…"

"In the truck?"

"Oh moon, yes. I've never had a girl in my truck."

"Oh."

"Mm-hmm. You're missing out," he teased.

"I want to say yes."

"Cheyenne, I'm teasing you. It's okay to take time. I want you to be sure. As long as you're not fighting me about everything just to spite me, I am happy."

"So. What about the full moon?" It was only a few days away, and it made his heart skip a beat to know she was thinking about him and the full moon, and not just with annoyance now.

"I'll just go to work. They're always looking for guys." He had a thought, hesitating for a brief moment before he asked, "Would you... stay here on the full moon?"

"Why?" She asked with narrowed eyes.

"Because it would make me feel better."

His mate pressed her lips together in a familiar look of suspicion, the lines of her mouth firming into her stubborn expression.

"Because I want nothing more than to bury myself inside of you and fuck you until you can't do anything but lie there and beg for mercy," he said, climbing on top of her.

Grabbing her wrists, he pinned her to the bed and kissed up her neck.

CHAPTER TWENTY-EIGHT

CHEYENNE

"*H*ey. Have you told them you're coming in tonight?"

"Yeah, why?"

"I want you to stay home with me." It was the first time she called it home.

"Okay. Baby, I want to, but I'm having a hard enough time right now. I don't trust myself to not…" he looked at her body, swallowing hard, crossing his arms over his chest, pressing his body into the corner.

"Then stay home with me," she replied, raising her eyebrows.

"No."

"Calen!" She said, looking around the room, then stalking to the bedroom. He followed her, only to get whacked in the face with a throw pillow the moment he entered the bedroom.

"Calen Merrick! You've harassed me for months, trying to get me to say yes, telling me that you'd fuck me if I gave you half a chance, and now you're backing out? Fuck me, or withdraw your claim on me." She challenged, gripping a second throw pillow, her wolf staring through her eyes at his.

"You are infuriating," he said, his voice low and husky.

"So are you. Are you serious about me? Or did you just want me to prove some kind of point, and now that I want you, you're ready to move on? Because if you're done with me, I'll go find some nice-"

"Cheyenne, don't," he warned.

"-boy to fuck my brains out tonight," she continued, her eyes narrowed in a challenge.

One moment she was standing next to the bed, the next she was flattened on it, trapped beneath his weight.

"Why are you always so *frustrating?*" He growled.

"Because you always have to have things your way, and that's not how I roll," she retorted.

"You're the same way!" He objected

"You picked me, sir!"

"Yes. And I'm going to keep picking you forever until one of us dies."

"Well, just know it's going to be you who goes first," she informed him.

"Damn right, it is. Because you won't have my permission to die first." He gave a smug nod and then kissed her as she struggled against him.

"You make me crazy," she began, but he kissed her again until she stopped.

"Now, if you're done arguing with me. Will you do me the honor of accepting my claim and allow me to court you exclusively?" He expected her to tease him, but she nodded and then pulled him in for another kiss.

"Yes. But you're not the boss of me," she said, after the kiss ended.

"Hm," he said in a noncommittal noise.

"Can we please have sex now?" She begged. "I want your dick in my mouth."

"That's one thing I'll never argue about," Calen said, unfastening his pants.

"Now get on your knees and put that smart mouth to good use. Suck my dick and don't stop until I fucking tell you," he ordered.

Hazel yipped with happiness, prompting Cheyenne to obey him

before he changed his mind about them. *The moon knows you made him work hard enough for it, show him how good we can be now!*

Cheyenne dropped to her knees and took him in her mouth, sucking on him eagerly without teasing him or easing into it. She'd been teasing him for months, and she wasn't going to make him wait any longer for his pleasure.

"Fuck, firecracker," he moaned, his fingers sliding into the hair behind her ear tenderly, his body shaking with the need to take her.

She took him as deep as she could, his cock hitting the back of her throat briefly before she backed off, bobbing on his length.

"You're too good at that," he said, using her hair to pull him out of her mouth.

"Are you telling me I'm overqualified?" She joked.

"Absolutely, you were about to make me a fifteen-second man, and we can't have that," he said. "No, you're getting the full package tonight, baby."

"Good," she purred, grinning at him.

"Take off those clothes, firecracker, or I'm going to take them off with my teeth," he threatened.

"Yes sir," she said, quickly stripping, but filing away the idea about him taking them off with his teeth for later.

"Calen," she breathed, "I want you."

"Sh," he said, covering her mouth.

Pushing her back against the bed, she frowned up at him, wondering why he didn't want her to say that she wanted him. He huffed a little at her expression and gave a slightly embarrassed smile.

"All I've wanted since that first morning when I rolled over and you were reading that smut was to make you scream my name, to alpha you in my bed until all you could do was lay there in a puddle. But, I sort of gave up on that and settled for just you wanting me after a while. Hearing you say it, just… it's everything."

She blushed and nodded.

"So you're saying if I tell you," she began, eyes bright as he lurched forward, covering her mouth.

"Mate," he said, his voice low. "I fully intend to take my time pleasing you. I've had every full moon for the last eight months to think about what I would do if it were me in your bed fucking you senseless, so don't fuck with me, hm? I can be nice to you and make you orgasm, or I can give you eight months worth of edging and teasing with you tied helpless to my bed. Your choice."

He removed his hand, giving her a raised eyebrow, waiting to see if she would challenge him. Cheyenne just nodded, her face crimson with pleasure and arousal.

"Good girl," he praised.

He made slow love to her, partially phasing to claim her with his knot. He took his time, pleasing her with mouth and fingers until she was unbearably aroused and begging for him to enter her. He positioned her on her knees on the bed, kneeling behind her to work his knot into her, stretching her slowly.

"Calen," she begged finally.

"Yeah?" He asked, his breath ragged.

"Just do it," she said.

"I'll hurt you," he said, shaking his head.

"I know," she said. "I want you to."

He pushed inside of her, his knot stretching her, her pussy resisting. Cheyenne relaxed as best as she could, and then he slipped inside and she screamed, her body contracting around him. Despite herself, she tried to scramble away from the pain, but he snatched her up, pulling her arm so his chest was to her back, keeping her impaled on his cock, and his knot.

"Oh no, firecracker, I've waited long enough to claim this pussy," he breathed into her ear his voice rough and ragged.

"Calen," she whimpered, the pain making her shiver.

"Tell me what you want now, my good girl," he said.

"I want..." she started to say, but broke off, too embarrassed to say it. "I can't. It's embarrassing. You'll make fun."

"Does it involve a clown suit or tapioca pudding and a bathtub?" He asked.

"What does that even mean?" Cheyenne said, laughing as she turned to face him.

"I promise not to make fun," he said solemnly.

"Swear?"

"Yes, Cheyenne, I swear. Now tell me, mate, what do you want?"

"I want you to ruin me for every other man who would ever want to fuck me," she whispered, her cheeks burning.

"With pleasure, firecracker."

CHAPTER TWENTY-NINE

CHEYENNE

*T*hey spent the rest of the afternoon and evening in bed, with a few brief breaks for a shower and some food. They'd made their way through the house, christening most of the surfaces, and making their way back to the bedroom.

"You know. If you'd have given me this much effort the first night, I'd have given you the time of day," Cheyenne informed him, giving him a sassy sideways grin.

"Really?" He asked idly, tracing his fingers over the skin of her soft stomach.

"Oh, definitely," she said.

"You like it when I'm bossy, huh?"

"I like it when you're in charge in the bedroom. I can't submit to someone who isn't really in charge. But you're getting better. You're almost halfway in charge now," she grinned mischievously.

He narrowed his eyes, sliding three fingers inside of her.

"Oh god."

"Not god baby. I own you. Now you cry out my name and pray I give you mercy. I'm going to fuck you so much tonight you won't be able to leave my bed tomorrow," he growled, thrusting roughly.

She wriggled on the bed, gripping his arm so her nails dug into his flesh, leaving little spots of blood.

"You want more?" He purred seductively.

"Yes!"

"Beg me," Calen ordered, slowing his assault.

She glared, matching his stare, pressing her lips together, not wanting to submit. Positioning himself between her legs, he stroked himself root to tip with one hand while his other hand stayed inside of her, sliding in and out slowly.

"Beg for my cock," he moved so his head rubbed on her swollen clit.

"Please, Calen. Please."

"What do you want?"

"Fuck me."

"Who's in charge?" he asked with a grin.

She tried to work up to being mad, but the way he rubbed against her felt too good.

"You."

"Who, baby?"

"You're in charge, damn it."

"You want me to fuck you with my fingers?"

"No!" She whined as he withdrew his fingers, positioning his tip at her entrance.

The full moon made every nerve sensitive, her entire body straining with the need to have him fill her with his seed. She tried to move her hips so he slid inside of her. It didn't matter how many times he'd had her, she needed more, as if this was the first time he'd touched her.

"Please give me your cock. Fuck my pussy and come inside of me. I need you." He slid in, her body giving no resistance, already dripping from their earlier lovemaking so he slid to the hilt easily. He lifted her legs to his shoulders, his balls slapping against her bottom as he thrust.

"Fuck," she cried out

"You are," his phone rang.

"Do you need to-" He covered her mouth with his hand, not slowing. The caller hung up, but called back immediately, hanging up after three rings. This repeated twice.

"WHOEVER IT IS, they better be dying." He snarled, pointing at her and ordering succinctly. "Stay."

He stood and rustled around to find his pants with his cell phone in the pocket.

"What?" He demanded furiously when he called back. He paused, his face draining "Oh fuck. On my way."

"What's wrong?"

"Work called me in."

"What's going on?"

"I've gotta go." He glanced at her regretfully. "Fire."

"Do you need to..." she spread her legs, eyebrows raised, giving his raging erection a significant look.

"I would have to be fast and I don't want to hurt you."

"I never asked you not to hurt me," she said alluringly as he pulled his clean work pants off the back of a chair.

One look at her and he was back on the bed, flipping her over so he could take her from behind. Gripping her hips so tight she cried out, he slammed into her so she surged forward, barely putting a hand out in time to keep her head from cracking into the headboard.

HE HADN'T BEEN KIDDING. She'd thought he'd been rough earlier, but now she thought he would bruise her. Not that she was complaining, far from it.

She felt her orgasm building, but he snarled, "Don't you fucking come yet."

She froze, trying to hold off, whining loudly.

"Please-" she was panting, her body breaking out into a sheen of sweat.

She felt him growing inside of her, his cock gaining almost a hand's length. She grasped the bedsheets as he assaulted her, pounding into her pussy with almost a rage when she felt something large bump against her entrance. The surprise was nearly enough to bring her back from the edge as alarm and curiosity brought back her rational mind to the surface.

Reaching between her legs, she touched his knot. "Oh, Calen."

"You're taking all of it," he informed her.

"You'll hurt me," she said, eyes growing wide. Taking his knot once when she was first aroused and very wet was one thing, but after a day full of sex, she was tender and already ready to be finished for a few more hours at least.

"You never asked me not to," he reminded her, putting long stead pressure, straining his hips as he pulled against her with his hands. She screamed as he slipped inside, trying to scramble away in panic.

"Stay," he ordered, his voice ringing with the authority of an alpha, and something else that made her insides warm that had nothing to do with the sex. She stilled and he stroked her back, him equally still inside of her.

"Good girl," he praised, panting slightly. They stayed there until she relaxed, breathing through the pain.

"I'm going to move."

"You'll kill me," she whimpered and he surprised her by chuckling darkly.

"Then you'll die mine." He started moving in little thrusts. "Come for me, Cheyenne."

"I can't."

"I wasn't asking." She slid her hands between her thighs, rubbing herself. Immediately she felt her orgasm building so hard her head spun.

"Good girl, just like that." He grabbed her hips again, his thrusts a little deeper so his tip brushed her cervix.

"Calen," She gasped, her entire body pausing for a moment except her hand.

He growled as she clamped down on him. His own orgasm had him thrusting in so hard he flattened her against the mattress, uttering a primal cry as she felt his enormous cock pulsing as he filled her, his knot pulsating, his warmth spreading through her. She screamed again, straining as the pleasure was almost overwhelming. His body weight held her down, every movement she made forcing his cock to move inside of her, heightening her pleasure.

"That's right baby."

He growled when she stopped moving, thrusting again. He'd come already, but she felt so incredible, the primal need to mark her as his in every way was so strong, that he kept thrusting even after his knot was beginning to shrink. She yelped when he bit the bundle of nerves between her neck and shoulder, then kissing her back as he rutted into her.

"Oh god." She shook against the mattress, the enormity of what they'd done making it through her fuzzy brain. He'd imprinted on her and she'd accepted him, completely. Cheyenne was truly his, and somehow it hadn't seemed real until he had fucked her without restraint. She panicked, trying to move away, but he took her shoulders, shushing her as he nuzzled her hair while she felt her own mating bond snap into place.

"Stop, or you'll hurt us." She wasn't sure if he meant him and her, or him and his wolf, but she stopped. "Give it a minute, baby."

"There's an emergency," she reminded him, even though she was more consumed with her own panic as she felt her own mating bond.

"Oh shit." In the heat of the moment he'd forgotten. "Take a deep breath and relax."

"I can't," she replied, almost in tears.

He nuzzled her neck, covering it with tender kisses, then moving to her shoulder.

"Relax for me," he said, lacing the words with his authority. It made her shiver as he slid out of her, his still swollen knot making her cry out as it stretched her sore entrance, releasing a rush of their fluids.

"I have to go," he murmured, and his heavy presence was gone from the bed.

"Okay," tears pricked her eyes, and she hid them in the pillow.

She'd never minded a man leaving her bed, but now she felt abandoned. Asking for permission to court her was an enormous thing, but imprinting was for life. Nothing undid it. They were joined together now, and he was leaving. Her wolf cried pitifully.

"Oh baby, don't cry." She hadn't realized she was making noise.

"I'm s-s-sorry," she cried even harder as he abandoned his effort to dress to come back to the bed.

"No, I can't leave if you cry, and I really have to go. There was a fire at the hotel."

"What? Oh my god." The hotel was always full of people mating for the full moon, and here she was moping about her first responder mate leaving their bed.

"Yeah."

"I'm coming," she said, rising from the bed, mindful of her surgery incision.

"No," he pulled on his work shirt.

"They'll need people to volunteer," she winced as her sore parts brushed against the fabric of her panties.

"You're not going anywhere, get back in bed," he ordered.

When she turned around to glare at him, incensed that he would dare try to leave her behind when there were people who needed help, she was surprised to find he was almost completely dressed.

"I'm part of the community too," she snapped. "I can't fight fires or do medic stuff but I can help scared people, and I'm good at what I do."

She shook her head and gave him an indignant sniff, looking for her clothes, finding her pants slung over the back of the couch and her shirt on the kitchen table.

"I know. It's that," he looked at her as she rushed around grabbing her clothes, "They'll... look at you."

Calen looked a little sheepish as he watched her dress, running his finger through his disheveled hair.

"Who will?"

"Other people," he replied.

"What are you talking about?"

"Other men. They'll look at you."

Cheyenne stopped to stare at him, irritation flaring inside of her.

"Oh my god. Seriously? Get a grip," she snapped. "There's an emergency. People are dying. I have I don't even know how many loads of your cum currently making a puddle in my panties. I'm going to be walking around like your personal whore, so even if they do look at me, it won't fucking matter. Pull your head out of your ass."

"Right." He shook his head, "Right, okay."

He watched her dress, sighing as he slid his belt on, heading to get his boots.

He came back to grab a large hoodie out of the closet, handing it to her as she dragged her t-shirt over her head.

"Wear that," he ordered, his tone brooking no argument.

"Okay." She accepted the hoodie with a little chuckle.

"Let's roll."

She grabbed a pair of his socks from his drawer, then her shoes on the way out. As an afterthought, she ran back and grabbed the bag of food from the fridge.

Climbing into the cab of the truck, she handed him some pieces of bacon from the container.

"Eat," she ordered.

"Gods I love you," he said with feeling.

She hummed happily, Hazel wagging her tail mentally as Calen offered her a piece of his bacon.

"I'm sorry, this isn't how I wanted this to go when we made things official," he said as they pulled up into the chaos that was the community center.

"It's okay, really. Just - don't get weird, okay? I'm yours, and even if I talk to someone else, it doesn't mean anything, okay?"

"Okay," he agreed.

CHAPTER THIRTY

CALEN

"Good, you're here," Ryder said shortly, "Cheyenne, they need help in the kitchen-"

"Don't tell her what to do," Calen snarled.

"Cool it, Merrick," Ryder said blandly, looking at his list.

"Tell her what to do again and we'll have a problem," Calen snarled, grabbing Cheyenne's arm to pull her behind him despite her protests.

Ryder narrowed his eyes in a challenge, then looked between the two of them, seeing something in Calen's eyes that made the corner of his mouth turn up.

"Congratulations. Cheyenne, would you please stay with the triage table and help keep them stocked? Here's a key for the supply closet, get them whatever they need. Grab a shirt for her if you want, so no one stops her."

"Mmkay," Calen said shortly.

"I'm sorry," Cheyenne said, mortified.

"Don't be. Been there myself." Ryder smiled and offered her a knowing wink.

. . .

THEY WORKED side by side through the night and well into the morning. She left to go get them coffee as he tended to a sprained ankle. When she came back, he dragged her to a quiet corner of the supply room, draining the coffee then hers.

"Hey!"

"I'll get you more. Right now, I need to do this." He pushed her into the wall with his body weight, trapping her in. She ducked her head when he tried to kiss her. "Not here,"

"Just one kiss," he begged.

"No-" she laughed, putting a restraining head on his chest. "You're working."

"Not anymore."

"Merrick?" Ryder asked opening the supply room door.

"Yeah."

"You can take Cheyenne back to the house, you're done."

"Thanks." Calen didn't move or turn from Cheyenne, eyeing her with a predatory gleam that made her wolf

"Merrick- no fucking in the supply closet. There are too many people around tonight."

Calen grunted, trying to kiss Cheyenne again.

"Hey!" Ryder said sharply.

"What?" Calen rounded in him, face dark.

"Go home," Ryder said. Calen's head cocked to the side, but Ryder stood his ground. "Put your wolf away, medic. Take your woman home, she's tired."

Calen looked around at Cheyenne's face, pale with exhaustion as she watched the interaction.

"Shut up, Ryder."

Ryder chuckled and gave Cheyenne a raise of one eyebrow to see if she needed help. Cheyenne shook her head and Ryder left them with a chuckle.

"You can't talk to him like that," she said softly to Calen once Ryder left.

"The hell I can't. Come on, let's get you into bed."

He drive her home, carrying her into the house despite her protests. She sat on the bed, too tired to remove her clothing.

"Let me."

"Don't get any ideas," she warned.

He just grinned as he tugged pulled the waist of her jeans, helping her to stand before pulling down her underwear and jeans in one motion, pushing her back into the bed with one hand on her abdomen so he could slip everything off. She left her T-shirt on, too tired to move.

"WANT THIS?" He returned with a T-shirt.

"Yeah." He dressed her, then flipped her around in the bed, stripping himself before climbing into bed.

"Do you need anything?" He asked, covering her with a blanket.

"You," she said sleepily. With a noise of pleasure, he moved against her, pulling her to him.

"That isn't what I meant," she grumbled.

"You don't want this?" He slid a hand between her legs, sliding his fingers inside of her. She winced, drawing away.

"You keep that thing away from me," she grumbled, but her smell changed as her body roused.

"If that's really what you want," he said, removing his fingers and snuggling behind her, nuzzling his nose in her neck.

She ground against him, snuggling and

"Just be gentle?"

"I will be," he promised, pressing a gentle kiss on her lips.

Sliding inside of her, he said in her ear, "This was all I've been thinking about since the last time I was inside of you."

"All?"

"Yes," he shuddered, moving slowly in and out of her.

"I guess I'm stuck with you now," she said with a soft laugh.

"I guess you are," he said, laying on top of her, not moving. His eyes searched hers, suddenly anxious. "You don't mind-" She put her hand to his cheek smiling softly.

"I don't mind,"

"Good. Because there's no take backs." He replied with a grin.

And just like that, she was his.

THE END

If you enjoyed this book, please leave a rating and review for Unwilling and Defiant with your favorite retailer. Reviews and ratings are the lifeblood of indie authors like me, and it would mean the world to me! Thanks so much!

www.ingramcontent.com/pod-product-compliance
Lightning Source LLC
Chambersburg PA
CBHW060349180626
46817CB00008B/2961